One Point Two Billion

One Point Two Billion

Stories

Mahesh Rao

4th

An Imprint of HarperCollins *Publishers*

First published in India in 2015 by Fourth Estate
An imprint of HarperCollins *Publishers*
A-75, Sector 57, Noida, Uttar Pradesh 201301, India
www.harpercollins.co.in

1 2 3 4 5 6 7 8 9 10

P-ISBN: 978-93-5177-484-6
E-ISBN: 978-93-5177-485-3

Typeset in 11.5/15 Electra LT Std Regular at
Manipal Digital Systems, Manipal

Printed and bound in India by
Replika Press Pvt. Ltd.

For my friend,
K.J. ORR

Contents

Eternal Bliss	1
Drums	20
The Agony of Leaves	34
The Trouble with Dining Out	53
Golden Ladder	68
Hero	94
The Pool	113
The Philanderer	131
Suzie Baby	149
The Earth Is Flat	164
Minu Goyari Day	181
The Word Thieves	203
Fizz Pop Aah	222
Acknowledgements	242
Notes and additional copyright information	244

ETERNAL BLISS

Bindu worried. She did not discriminate and gave freely of her time to trifling inconveniences as well as insurmountable predicaments. She tended her anxieties well, ready with kindling when their flame died down – an unlikely consequence here, a remote disaster there. Two lines had formed across her forehead in recent months and she worried about them too.

The biggest worry of all had been whether she would get the job at the Paramasukha International Yoga Centre. Nervousness had upset her stomach the morning of the interview and she had nearly called to cancel. But her savings had dwindled to almost nothing and that thought had been terrifying enough to spur her on to the suburban bus stand, fortified by three different types of antacid.

At the interview she had lied and said that she was a widow. She had felt that her status as a woman separated from her husband would sit uncomfortably in a place of such spirituality, whereas a tragic death in her near past would be embraced. After getting the job, she had begun to fret about what would happen if her employers came to know the truth: that her husband had not been borne away by the waters of the Kaveri but was, in fact, managing a tyre factory in Tumkur.

The yoga centre was situated fifteen kilometres outside Mysore, amid orchards of coconut and mango trees. Its nearest neighbours were a scooter repair shop and a factory that manufactured water tanks. The centre could accommodate thirty guests in small rooms that were clean but gloomy, even when the daylight outside dazzled like white metal. There were two teachers: Shashi, a tiny man with a voice like a flute, and Gopal, whose T-shirts blazed the letters of his name, as though he were a football star. Alcohol and drugs were strictly prohibited in all parts of the premises. Cigarettes had been included in this ban too, but in the face of falling occupancy numbers the prohibition had been lifted.

Bindu was the centre manager. Her duties were diverse and caused her a great deal of anxiety, but her previous job had been worse. She had worked in a hotel in

Bangalore, wedged into a corner of Majestic, dealing with uncouth businessmen and their mistresses, all boss-eyed with alcohol. The yoga centre was a great improvement. The foreigners' behaviour was at times incomprehensible but at least they were incredibly polite. They thanked her three times for getting someone to bring them a cup of warm water.

On her second day a woman from Los Angeles had arrived at the centre, saying that she wanted to become a Brahmin.

Bindu had creased her brow and said: 'I am very sorry, madam, but we are not running such classes.'

'Oh sure, I know that. But after the yoga, that's where I want to be at.'

Clumps of marigolds lined the pathways that led to the thatched dining room, the residential block and a structure referred to as 'the spa'. This was a long, low room divided by a sagging wall into male and female treatment areas. Therapeutic massages were provided here by Thomas and Rosa, a married couple whose last civil words to each other were uttered years ago. They kept to their respective areas during the day, meeting only for silent meals, which they took at opposite ends of the staff kitchen. At night they lay on their massage beds, each listening out for the other's snores behind the partition wall, their jaws tight with repressed rage.

The circular from the Department of Culture arrived late in the afternoon. The officials at the Directorate of Spiritual Affairs (DoSA) would be making their annual inspections in the weeks to come. All licensed institutes of spiritual practice and moral disciplines were required to ensure that their facilities and procedures met the approved government standards. Ample notice was provided to all relevant parties as DoSA seemed to recognize that superintendence by ambush served no one, least of all their inspectors, who had become accustomed to a level of comfort that could seldom be provided at short notice.

A rush of nausea assailed Bindu. The responsibilities of her job had been taking their toll. At night a stubborn cinder burnt its way through her stomach and in the morning her neck was tense and achy. She had taken to drinking large quantities of milk to cool her insides but had begun to put on weight and was plagued by indigestion. And now important government officials would descend on the centre, piling out of cars with sirens, pens ranged in their pockets. They would peer into files, look under beds, question the guests and sniff the air for signs of degeneracy.

'Don't worry, madam,' said Santhosh, the assistant manager, a man in his late twenties, on the cusp of running to fat. 'They will just stamp this paper, fix that seal, have lunch and go. We have already paid for the licence so what else is there for them to do?'

'It's an inspection, Santhosh. They will inspect. Have you seen the state of the kitchen today? And the laundry has not been done since Tuesday. And that American lady is being a Brahmin on the grass that we have just planted. Go and do something.'

Santhosh sighed and made his way towards the kitchen. He saw little value in being overly zealous in his duties – he knew that he was destined for better things. He had overheard snatches of conversation between guests discussing the transformative nature of their spiritual experiences at the centre. Santhosh was unsure what it all meant, but had concluded that he had transformative powers too. He was the second in command in a place that attracted people who were much more worldly and educated than him. They must have, therefore, recognized something special about him. He wondered whether he was the reincarnation of an important historical figure. Unable to decide but keen to distinguish himself, he had taken a loan and bought a new motorbike.

It was easy to spot the guests who were keen to learn. They competed to place their mats in the front row of the hall and were arriving for classes ever earlier. They would stay late after class too, engaging the teachers in conversation, making detailed enquiries as to sequence, breath counts and curvature. Bindu heard one of them ask Gopal about the route to liberating the eternal self. She had no idea what it involved, but was quite sure that Gopal, who was known to beat his wife with a chappal, was not the man to ask.

A few of the guests had been at the centre for months and showed no indication of leaving. Adam was one of them. He owned a second-hand car showroom in Manchester and it was not clear to Bindu who was running it in his absence. Adam's attendance at classes was commendable and in the afternoons he meditated on the front lawn in a lungi, a frangipani blossom tucked behind his right ear.

'You have a beautiful Indian face,' he said to Bindu one day.

She was not sure whether he meant that her face was beautiful in spite of being Indian or that it was so un-Indian, and yet beautiful, that both she and he needed to be reminded of its Indianness.

She smiled and said: 'Thank you.'

Another long-term guest was Mathilde from Switzerland. Her animated conversations over dinner often resulted in her glass bangles breaking as they struck the table, and she would replace them on frequent trips to Mysore. Mathilde enjoyed providing instructions and advice to her fellow guests. On days when her yoga practice had been particularly fulfilling, she was even more garrulous. Her main areas of expertise were temple etiquette, stray dogs and the principles of effective bargaining. She was the only guest who had managed to evoke a troubled antipathy in Bindu. Mathilde had a tendency to appear in the reception area when Bindu was registering new guests, her darting eyes aglow with the urge to facilitate. Bindu was not normally a territorial woman, but had recently taken to welcoming new arrivals in a secluded spot under a jackfruit tree.

Between yoga sessions there seemed to be little to occupy the guests and Bindu sometimes worried that in moments of idleness they would get together and formulate complaints about her work. So when Santhosh suggested that they organize a few day trips, she agreed gladly. Excursions were arranged to the Ranganathittu Bird Sanctuary and to Tipu Sultan's summer palace in Srirangapatna. Santhosh had also heard that some of the guests were eager to become active in the community by doing some voluntary work. Without consulting Bindu, he arranged for a minibus to transport a few guests to a nearby orphanage. He presumed that the children, some of whom had escaped deeply traumatic situations, would enjoy a bit of novelty in their routine.

The trip was a disaster. The sight of so many strangers, some of them well over six feet tall with shaved heads and tattoos, unsettled the children and one of them suffered a fit. The foreigners returned to the centre, crestfallen and exhausted. Bindu felt compelled to give Santhosh a formal warning.

A second circular arrived from the Department of Culture, accompanied by a fat annexe of questionnaires seeking details of the centre's policies on austerity, abstinence, purity, devotion and abstraction.

Bindu pushed her chair away from the desk as if the letter had the capacity to cause a physical injury. Then she crammed it into a folder, which she then locked in the safe. Her first instinct was to avoid the inspection altogether by pretending to be ill around the time the officials were expected – but she knew if she did that her lies would be discovered and she would lose her job.

She wondered if she too should try yoga. The centre's guests all said that it brought them a profound serenity and there was nothing in life that she desired more. She was too embarrassed to join the guests at their classes so she begged Gopal to give her a few private lessons on the kitchen veranda. After squeezing various rota-related concessions out of her, he finally agreed.

The sessions brought no serenity. Gopal barked intermittent instructions at her while looking at price comparison websites on his phone. Even though he had no intention of purchasing a water purifier or a washing machine, he was the sort of man who liked to be well informed.

Bindu persevered. Her hips creaked during surya-namaskara, her arms felt feeble, and in the end she lost her balance, nearly toppling onto the veranda steps. In trikonasana the blood rushed to her head and she felt as though it might explode. When she tried to lift her legs into sarvangasana, palpitations rocked her chest. She had seen the contortions of the more experienced practitioners and a fear began to torment her. What if she tore a muscle, what if her spine snapped, what if she hit her head and lost her mind? She had recently read a disturbing article about brain injuries that resulted in patients believing that they were in the process of turning into an animal, most commonly a wolf or a monkey.

The classes were discontinued and Bindu doubled her dosage of sleeping pills.

There were several maids employed at the centre. Manjula was the longest serving and the most astute. She had a wiry body but a fleshy face, a mouth filled with dark, pitted teeth and sported a bindi the size of a two-rupee coin. Her grey hair was gathered in a loose bun, which always looked on the point of collapse but never succumbed. She spent the majority of her time trying to wring as much as she could out of the centre's guests. At work she only wore saris the colour of dirt and made sure that the holes in her blouses were visible. She had learnt a handful of words in English: 'pain', 'baby crying', 'tired', 'sad' and 'butter'. Most gave at least twenty rupees, especially newcomers.

Some years ago a guest from Wisconsin had given Manjula a five-dollar note. Being new to such gifts at the time, she had not known how to have it exchanged. So she had framed the note and propped it up in her shrine among the pictures of gods and saints. Along with Shiva, Ganesha and Sai Baba, her daily rituals came to involve Abraham Lincoln too.

She now had nearly enough saved to purchase a fridge. She had already gone into the city three times to have a look at the one she wanted. It was gunmetal-grey, had three shelves, a freezer compartment and a total capacity of 165 litres. In the summer, she planned to keep handkerchiefs in the freezer and then lay them over her face at night.

Srinivasa was the day watchman. His main tasks included patrolling the grounds, directing guests to the reception and chasing away any local youth who came to ogle foreign women. Srinivasa was civil to the hotel guests but no more. He was suspicious of people who would leave their countries – places where buses left on time, power and water flowed without interruption, and policemen genuinely apprehended criminals – in order to exercise together in a hall. In particular, he had taken exception to Adam and his penchant for ostentatious chanting on the front lawn. He made sure to keep an eye on him.

Srinivasa and Manjula regularly argued about the foreigners.

'You should be ashamed of yourself,' he said to her one day, 'feeding on their scraps like a dog.'

'You are the filthy, diseased dog,' she responded. 'If it wasn't for them, you wouldn't have a job and your wife would be selling herself fifty times a day. Keep complaining, you wait and see, your children will starve to death and your wife will leave you for a man with a thunne big enough to satisfy her.'

'You leave my family out of this. We all have self-respect. We don't come to work in rags, hoping for a few coins of charity.'

Manjula smiled sweetly. 'When your thunne shrivels up completely and drops off, I will help you bury it in a ditch.'

Bindu was unaware of these tensions between the members of her staff. Her focus continued to be the centre's guests and she did everything that she could to make them comfortable. A recent arrival was Dafna from Tel Aviv. She had decided to travel to India in spite of her mild agoraphobia. Soon after her arrival she had spotted two men defecating in a playground, a sight that had severely aggravated her condition. Since arriving at the yoga centre, she had not left her room. Bindu made sure her breakfast, lunch and dinner were taken to her. The poor woman had paid for them, after all.

A greater concern was Sue from London. She changed into a floral bikini and lay in the sun all afternoon in spite of the numerous signs around the property requesting guests to kindly maintain decorous attire at all times. Bindu did not know what to do. She disliked confrontations of any kind and had never had one with a foreigner. There had been a near miss a few months ago with a mother and daughter from Australia. They had hardly attended any classes and one of the maids had said that she had seen them in their room, drinking Old Monk rum first thing in the morning with the man who worked in the scooter repair shop. Bindu had been about to call the owners to ask for their assistance when the mother and daughter had walked into the reception area, asking for their luggage to be stored until further notice. They had left on the back of the repairman's scooter as Bindu waved them off, instantly worrying about whether they would return.

Another guest, Mr Anderson, was a thickset gentleman from New York. Bindu noticed three days after his arrival that he was greeting everyone with an ornate bow. She assumed it was something they did where he came from. A couple of days later, he approached her at reception.

'You know, Bindi,' he said, 'everything here is so different, so pure. I don't know how to explain it.'

Bindu nodded, wondering if this was a precursor to an official complaint.

'It has really made me think about so many aspects of my life back home and all the places where I was going wrong. I feel like I'm questioning everything. Do you see, Bindi? Everything.'

Bindu nodded again, still not sure if the things Mr Anderson was questioning included the quality of the service at the centre.

'You make so many assumptions, you just go on and on, never really thinking, never really searching, and then one day, you're sixty. Just like that.'

'Is the geyser in your bathroom okay, sir? Are you getting hot water?'

'What? Oh sure, that's fine. What was I saying? Yes, life just happens to you and you just let it happen, you walk the dog, you watch the game, you get married, you get divorced, you get married again, you get divorced again, your dog dies, you get a new dog, and all that time, like a blind man, just never really see anything at all. You know what I mean, Bindi?'

Bindu had frozen at the mention of divorce, her innards taking a tumble. How had a man recently arrived from America stumbled upon the facts of her precarious marital status? She listened more intently but did not dare look him in the eye.

Instead, she focused on the large floral print on his shirt and said, 'Yes, sir.'

Mr Anderson wandered off and Bindu balled her fists in her lap. He seemed like a sympathetic man, a gentle stranger who would not involve himself in the intimate affairs of others. She looked up to see him standing at the far end of the garden, apparently admiring a bee. Mildly reassured, she returned to a problem involving the purchase of the wrong type of light bulbs.

There was a third letter from the Department of Culture the following day. Addressees were reminded that any attempt to hinder DoSA officials from full execution of their duties would result in the most severe sanctions. For the avoidance of all doubt, the letter reproduced lengthy tracts from several statutes.

As Bindu tried to decipher the clauses, hunched over the reception desk, Adam chided her for her posture and offered to give her a shoulder massage. She pretended not to hear him. A few days later, he gave her a present, a little token, he said, to cheer her up: a bound set of illustrations of the erotic sculptures at Khajuraho. This only raised her pulse rate, already dangerously high. She was concerned that she would be accused of improper behaviour with a guest, and spent the good part of an afternoon ripping pages from the book, which she then stashed with the DoSA circular in the safe.

There were other troubles too. Petty cash had gone missing and she needed to find out who was to blame. Two maids had left, following an altercation with Manjula. There had been a grouse about the quality of the evening meals. The latest blow was that one of the guests had sprained her shoulder and had asked to see an osteopath, confusing Santhosh who thought that she required an astrologer.

At night, Bindu waited for sleep, the difficulties of the day spooling through her mind. Images of her ex-husband broke through, forcing her eyes open: a lolloping dance he would employ to soften her up; his broad back, slick with sweat; the curl of stubble that he always missed shaving. Perhaps she ought to beg his forgiveness for abandoning him, plead with him to take her back. Then a surge of hurt and humiliation washed back in and she took a couple of sleeping pills, worrying about addiction.

The DoSA officials arrived on a Monday morning, a week later than expected. Bindu had expected a convoy to screech to a halt in the car park and all exits from the centre to be blocked by surly guards. But instead, a matronly woman and diminutive man descended from a rickshaw, their car having irremediably sunk into a pothole outside Nanjangud.

'I am S.G. Chithralekha, Second Assistant Chief Inspector, DoSA,' said the woman, the glare of her fuchsia sari adding to the harsh brilliance of her eyes.

Suspended on various chains and cords, a number of items had come to rest on the massive shelf of her bosom: reading glasses, an amulet, a phone and a locket. The strings of jasmine in her hair looked like they dared not wilt, no matter how hot the day.

S.G. Chithralekha's gaze was drawn at once to Adam's fervent incantations on the front lawn.

'Who is that man?' she asked.

'One of our guests,' said Bindu, trying to guide her towards the reception desk, 'a very studious and humble man. He has a big second-hand car dealership in England, but look how simply and spiritually he is dressed.'

S.G. Chithralekha offered no comment and gestured to her male assistant to follow them. She made no attempt to introduce him and he did not appear to expect otherwise.

Bindu had not been expecting a woman. A woman would intuit the shortcomings of the centre, especially a woman like S.G. Chithralekha. With one look at Thomas and Rosa, she would discern the toxic atmosphere in the spa; she would sense the terror seeping out of agoraphobic Dafna's room; she would suspect that Gopal had surreptitiously been taking photos of female guests and see that the centre's accounts were as fanciful as its testimonials.

The centre owners pulled up in the car park at that moment. They had chosen to arrive in a battered Maruti 800, borrowed from a lesser branch of the family, rather than in one of their SUVs. It was best not to give these government officials the wrong idea. Further introductions were made and the two DoSA officials were taken to observe a meditation class and to interview the yoga teachers.

Bindu had begun to walk up the path to make sure the storerooms were tidy when she saw Manjula running towards her, sari hitched up in one hand, a duster fluttering in the other.

'Bindu madam,' she panted, 'he's dead.'

'Who? What are you talking about?'

'The big man from America. I went to clean his room now and I saw him. Finished.'

This was the abridged version. Manjula had knocked on Mr Anderson's door, and hearing no response, had gone in using her key. His body lay on the bedspread, stiff and solid, one arm aimed at the skirting board. She had known instantly that he was dead. Spotting his trousers folded over a chair, she had gone through the pockets. In his wallet there was a picture of a woman and a teenaged boy, their round faces shimmering like Kashmiri apples. Manjula had extracted a thousand rupees and fifty dollars and slipped the wallet back into the man's trousers. These days she knew not only where to change foreign currency, but which dealer offered the best rates. After hiding the money behind a loose brick in the kitchen wall, she had raised the alarm.

In spite of Santhosh's efforts to delay the DoSA officials at the spa, when the police arrived S.G. Chithralekha was watching with great interest and making notes in a diary. Her assistant sat on a sack of rice, his head in his hands.

A short while later, members of the local press made an appearance.

One reporter planted himself in front of Bindu.

'How did he die? Drugs?' he asked eagerly.

'Drugs are strictly prohibited in every part of the yoga centre,' said Bindu, trying to make her way past him.

'You can say off the record, madam. Overdose?' he persisted.

Bindu wanted to weep. Events had taken such a devastating turn that they had bested her most pessimistic forecasts. She turned away from the reporter and tried to find a quiet spot where she could bring some order to her thoughts.

At the entrance to the spa Thomas and Rosa watched the melee, their faces expressionless. Rosa ate a banana, swirling and sucking on each mouthful until it slipped down her throat. When she finished, she tossed the peel into the air and went back inside. The peel landed on Thomas's feet.

After the last policeman had left, Srinivasa shut the gates. He thought about the dead man who had come all the way to India from America and was now being taken to an overcrowded morgue where he would probably languish for weeks.

He said to Manjula: 'This has happened because of you. Your thieving and lying has visited this upon all of us. Even your shadow is inauspicious.'

'I hope maggots eat your brain from the inside out and that your screams are heard in the furthest corners of hell,' she said.

As Bindu tried to calm anxious guests, she wondered whether she had failed Mr Anderson in some way. He had wanted to tell her something about his life but she had not been able to penetrate his hazy commentary. She sat down on a stool behind the front desk, trying to recall his exact words, her head in the crook of her elbow. When the first guests began to stream past to the dining room for dinner, she did not notice.

She was convinced that the DoSA officials would initiate investigations into the death of her husband. S.G. Chithralekha seemed precisely the kind of person who would make a couple of phone calls to senior bureaucrats and discover in a matter of hours that Bindu's husband was not only alive but flourishing in the vulcanized rubber industry. Was it illegal to claim a widowhood that one had not yet attained? Bindu did not know. And now there had actually been a death at the centre. In the world's eyes, Bindu's crimes would be piling up.

There seemed to be only one option. The next day, she called the centre owners and told them that she was returning to Bangalore. They begged her to reconsider but she told them that she had already accepted another job offer.

The DoSA preliminary report arrived on the day Bindu left for Bangalore. The report had been expedited as a result of the tragic death of Mr Anderson and a cash incentive offered to Ms Chithralekha by the centre owners. Its conclusions were unequivocal. The

Paramasukha International Yoga Centre had proved itself to be an unrivalled provider of spiritual sustenance. The quality of instruction was faultless and its value was only enhanced by the transcendental environment in which it was delivered. The coffee was also delicious.

The inspectors had been amazed to note that during their brief visit, one of the centre's guests had been so committed to selfless devotion and contemplation that he had departed his corporeal form and achieved enlightenment while they were having their lunch. What better illustration could there be of the centre's phenomenal success?

That evening, Bindu got off the bus at Majestic. The wheels had come off her suitcase and she had some trouble dragging it along the uneven paving stones, past the bus conductors, the touts and the hawkers. She waited at the traffic lights and looked at the circuit of jagged concrete: the sweep of the overpass, the cracked stanchions, the buildings that warped into each other. At the next corner stood the hotel where she had worked. The management had agreed to take her on again, but at slightly reduced wages.

DRUMS

I never knew women could make such noises. All around me their snores are rising like the voices of demons. See, that feeble girl near my feet sounds as if she is trying to climb out of her grave. And somewhere at the back of the tent, the worst of all, a she-spirit howling for salvation. Who knows what kind of sleep this is? I would have been happier to be thrown into one of the tents with all the men. None of them would want to touch me. And their spit-wet growling would not make my chest heave like the din from these troublesome slatterns all around me.

Next to me, a woman is awake.

'One or two more days,' she says to her child. 'Then we will go home.'

'Why are you lying to her?' I ask.

The woman tucks the girl's head deep into her bosom and shrugs away from me.

'You.' I touch her neck.

The woman's head snaps towards me. 'Be quiet.'

'Why are you lying to the girl? You are not going anywhere.'

'If you don't know anything, stop talking.'

'Know what?'

'The camp is closing tomorrow or the day after. They are moving us somewhere else.'

'Where?'

She lowers her head and stays silent.

A few moments later she says, 'We will pack up our things and go.'

Pack up our things. My things are in a bundle I can feel against the bones in my back. There are two saris. There is a tin plate, a bead necklace and a towel. A hundred-rupee note is stitched into the hem of a rag.

If we are leaving in one or two days, that is not much time. God save me, I have no idea where we will end up. If they will not take us back to the village, then where?

Sani is in this tent. Her presence is like a knife slicing into my palms. I have not spoken to her for more than thirty years, but I always know when she is nearby. I can count her breaths and guess where her foot is going to fall. I have known her all her life.

All those years ago, I ran her finger along a bamboo stalk, as smooth as a mirror. I told her we had to cut while the moon's crescent was young. I showed her the axe's blade with its perfect edge. I watched as she stood the culms in the sun. I helped her drag them into the shade. I sliced off the nodes and pared down their scars slowly, so she could see. I taught her to slit the ends open, drive a wedge into the stem and split the whole from its heart.

When she was unclean, I would sneak into the hut and feed her peanuts and honey. The following month, I would do it again.

I lined her eyes with kohl.

In return, Sani took my husband.

'You would not lie to an old woman.'

The men look up.

'Is it true that we are being moved from here tomorrow?'

They look at each other.

'Yes, we are going to a five-star hotel tomorrow. There will be one servant to scratch your head and one to scratch your feet,' says the one with a face like a bat.

'Please tell me, if you know anything. I beg you not to make fun of an old woman.'

'The government won't even give us two meals here. Where do you think they will take us?'

'To another camp?'

'A better one? One with sofas and TVs?'

The men laugh again.

I walk on.

Every morning and evening there is a roll call for all the men and boys in the camp. They line up outside the broken school building to be counted. As if any of these weaklings would escape. Beyond the barbed wire, there are only Naxalis, landmines and, over there in the distance, the forest. After roll call, the men leave to dig the road that seems to stretch endlessly. And they return when the sun is low to be counted again by the soldiers.

Sani's son is one of these men. Deva takes after her in every way. It is as if cakes of clay have been stripped off her face, arms and thighs and used to mould a young man. His eyes stare like hers, his forehead is narrow, his limbs are long. You won't believe, he even shrugs like her, one shoulder higher than the other. There is nothing of his father in him.

Deva pretends to be a respectful man, even though Sani's slyness must course through his veins too. He always bows his head when he sees me. During the day he disappears with the other men to work on the road, but he is back here in the evening. I see him walking through the camp or eating with his mother. Every time I say it: how alike they look. He used to bring me water in the village even though I never touched it. He would return without a sound for the pot. He has brought wood. He has tried to touch my feet. She makes him call me 'grandmother' even though she is only ten years younger than me and I was married to his father. She is a crafty witch; I have been seeing that all her life.

My mother said that I should go and see her baba. He would make my husband return. But I knew that no mantra, no sacrifice, no salve could take on the power of Sani's long lashes. He would return only if he wanted to. And he never did. He was killed by his own hand, a machete wound that ate him alive. He got what he deserved.

The fires have been lit. Their light softens this place, the faces lose their spite. I pass the groups looking at the glow and walk alongside the fence. I have come far from my tent. Here the ground is chalky, and dead fronds snap under my feet. There is hardly any moon tonight but I have good eyes. There are shadows that skip and twist ahead of me and I make my way towards them.

A group of men are standing with their backs to me. One of them hears me approach and spins around.

'What do you want?' he asks, stepping forward.

I beckon to him.

'Get away from here, what's wrong with you?' he hisses.

The men with him have decided that I am not worth bothering about and don't even turn around. I see that a crowd has formed in front of them and I push my way to the front. There is a thrashing of wings and the shine of white feathers. The men are preparing a pit for a cockfight. Even when they are caged in a camp, they have to scratch out their strength on a chicken's buttocks.

No women at the cockfights, they used to say in the village. You women will pour water on a fighter's flame. But I went once, dressed as a boy. The winning cock was a glorious creature, its plumes snatched from the night. As it moved forward, its red throat rose out of a breast of rock, its eye as vicious as its spur. The men were drunk with the power of what they were seeing. I smelt it in their sweat, saw it in their veins.

But the cocks by the side of this pit are ravaged little vermin. One is a speckled cripple with a stub of a comb. The other has a stomach the colour of shit. There is no roar here, no frenzy. The men rub the cocks' legs. See how they do it: each action stolen and sly. There are whispers and grumbles. A bundle of twigs rakes through the sand. There is a quick count and the cocks are let loose in the pit. Where is the roar? I swear to you, within seconds the cocks collide and collapse. The handler of the speckled cock pulls it back. He jolts it against his knee and then blasts smoke into its eyes. He releases the cock into the pit again but look at it, the runt just falls back into his arms.

I want to say to the men that this is what their manhood has become here. Two stunted cocks who don't even have the strength to bleed. I nudge my way back through the group.

A man standing on his own has been watching me. He doesn't look like the other men here, the kind who would sell you their mothers for a handful of mahua blossoms.

'Not wagering anything, grandmother?' he asks me.

'All I have is in my belly.'

'You have that at least.'

'How much do they pay you to work on the road?'

'Fifty rupees a day, if we are lucky.'

'So you must have a nice treasure hidden away.'

'Yes, why not, I shit gold coins every morning.'

'Someone told me they are closing the camp tomorrow and taking us somewhere else. What do you think, is it true?'

'Does a frog care whose foot crushes him, the ranger's or the poacher's? Even if you find out where we are going, what will you do?'

I chuckle.

'Do you have another beedi?'

He takes the one pressed between his lips and hands it to me. When I suck it, the tobacco hits me like a punch to the face.

Years ago, my husband took Sani to see the cave shrine near Badhgarh. I saw them leave, hurrying as the sun came up. I followed them. We walked the whole way, more than three hours, she a few paces behind him, and then a safe distance away, me. The three of us threaded through the forest, past the faces on the kusum trunks and the walls of moss. He merged with the trees and the soil; I could only hear his steps. But I never lost sight of her sari, a dark purple in the forest light. They only stopped to rest once, sitting on a fallen tree. I stood with my back to them, not wanting to see them at rest, listening instead for the sound of crushed leaves as they moved on.

When they reached the rock, I held back and watched them climb. He was strong and quick. I could see her struggle on the slope, her thigh quivered as it bore her weight. He pulled her up, grasping at her arm, her waist. When they reached the top, I could see them carved into the sky.

I went after them, taking two boulders at a time, jumping over clefts, tasting the salt from my sweat. I had made this journey many times before and I knew a route that was short but steep. It ended at a ridge that dipped towards the Badhgarh cave like an arrowhead. My feet in the smallest nooks, my fingers clawing at gravel, I must have pierced and grazed my skin dozens of times. At last I drew my body up over the edge.

I lay on the rock and caught my breath, its warmth seeping into my stomach. Below me, Sani and my husband stood under a mantel of stone. The sun was in my eyes but I swear I had never seen them more clearly. They stood still, looking in the direction of the entrance to the cave. Then he lowered her to the ground, leaned back against the rock and laid her head in his lap. I saw it for the last time, the tenderness of a man.

Only I know how I ran down that hill, sliding on scree, stumbling over roots. I reached the forest and the knots in the grasses whipped against my legs. Giant sprays of ferns slapped at my face. I could feel every groove and clump under my feet as I ran until my breath left me and I threw myself on to the ground. Clods of earth crumbled under my back as a teetar sent down its taunts from the branches above. I knew then that Sani was pregnant.

I can see Sani's form as I settle in my corner in the tent. She has a choice to go and sleep somewhere else. But she continues to take her place here. It is her way of letting me know that she has done nothing wrong. We are old, the hills are bare, the man is dead, our homes are embers. What else needs to happen? That is what she is asking me when she lies there.

Even in a place like this, there is music. The sound rises above the massive sal tree and enters the tent. I can hear the conversation of two drums. There is the bigger one, the male, pounding. Then there is the smaller female, resisting. Come, says the male drum, come closer. No, says the female drum, her beats sharper and softer. I think you should, says the male, persuading, insisting. No, says the female, but you can tell that her count is fading, her pulse becoming faint. At last, says the male, his rhythm the god. There is one last surge and then there is silence. Stupid bitch; she should have slapped him across the face with a broom.

A loose tent flap hangs above my head. I can see that daylight is still hours away. The night looks like it would rub off on my fingers and smear across my forehead. There are no stars any more in this place, just darkness. In the old days a river ran not far from our village. At night it showed us trails of light. Now the riverbed is a sewer and the moon has turned a rancid yellow.

The nephew of the sarpanch once stood in my path.

'Your heart must be happy,' he said.

'Why?'

'You have got what you wanted.'

'What did I want?'

'That this land should become like your womb.'

I took a slow breath and hawked into his face with all my force. The spit clung to the mole below his eye before he wiped it off. It was only when I was back in my hut that it felt like my bones had turned into water.

The refinery came first. It gouged into the land, tearing out its lungs. Its blood made the dust red and the angry wind sent that dust spiralling in every direction. In the middle of the night, rocks pushed up from the soil, strange shapes that menaced us like devils. Mynahs began to fall out of the air, drunk on some sweet vapour. The streams dived into underground caves, leaving only gullies of scum. The dawns were suddenly silent.

After that the Naxalis came.

Then the soldiers. When they arrived in the village, we were expecting them. It was not the first time they had come, called us from our homes, pushed us to the ground. This time, people had already patted soil tightly over their money, stuffed their tiny gold studs into the bend in a tree's roots. Those who could leave had left.

The soldiers said that the government wanted to protect us, we had to leave for our own good. If we stayed, the Naxalis would find us and drink our blood. They did not want the Naxalis to take over our village as a base. We were given five minutes to gather what we could before being loaded into the truck. I looked at the young girls around me, thought of myself at their age. It was their turn to demand and plot and rage. But they all sat like me, silent and sunk. As we moved away, I could smell smoke and see flecks of ash sail through the air. I didn't look back.

Now they have brought us to this place and, after all these years, I am lying a few feet away from Sani. In my bundle, a hundred-rupee note is stitched into the hem of a rag.

A soldier is sitting on a chair outside the school building, his legs stretched out on a blackened log. I creep forward and see that his eyes are closed.

'God give you a long life, son,' I say.

He opens one eye and looks at the gun in his lap, as if it is the one that spoke.

I shuffle forward and crouch at his feet.

He uncrosses his legs. One hand moves over the gun.

'With your help, I need to see the big man,' I say.

'Who?'

'Thanedaarji, inside.'

He opens both eyes and looks at the gun again. It is growing out of his groin.

'Why?'

'I have to talk to him.'

'I said why.'

'I have some information to give him.'

'Tell me, then we'll see.'

'Please, don't disappoint an old woman.'

He closes his eyes and his head falls slowly back again.

'Here.'

In my fist, my hundred-rupee note is folded into a diamond. I unclasp it.

He opens his eyes and sees the note. He grabs it like an eagle.

'Where did you get that?'

'I had it. It was mine.'

He laughs and crosses his legs again.

I have not lived for nothing. I settle down to wait at a respectful distance. There is a peacock feather in the mud at my feet. I look around. Two old men are bent over a bicycle lying on the ground. Another soldier is lying on a charpoy, asleep in the sun. A group of children are shooting arrows at a dog, chasing it as it tears through the long grass. No one seems to have noticed the feather. I pick it up, wipe its head with my thumb and tuck it into the folds of my sari.

The soldier uncrosses his legs and swings them off the log. Without looking at me, he stands up and walks into the school building. A few feet away, two men are digging a trench. The soil goes up into the air. What is the trench for; who ordered it? I can tell from their faces they do not know. But the soil must fly.

The soldier returns. He jerks his head at the building.

'Two minutes.'

I stand, bow to him, and dart in through the doorway.

The schoolroom glows like a temple full of lanterns. Through a hole in the roof, the evening light pours on to the floor. Pictures torn from magazines cover the bars on the windows; the last of the day's sun is sieved through the actresses' eyes, lips and breasts. The thanedaar is sitting on a desk in a checked shirt, his back straight. His uniform is slung across a line that sags behind him. His eyes are in darkness but his cheeks are craters as deep as mine. He is looking at the phone in his hand.

'No signal all day again,' he says.

I stare at him until he looks up.

'What do you want?' he asks.

'I have something important to tell you,' I say.

I let him see that my hand is shaking.

'What is it?'

I mumble: 'It's about a Naxali.'

He stands up and beckons me closer. His eyes are the colour of dirty water.

I step forward and sit on my haunches, even though the pain is unbearable.

He bends towards me.

I hope to remind him of his grandmother. I give him a sad, kind smile and I whisper.

I crawl out of the tent at first light and make my way to the centre of the camp. I wrap my sheet around me and crouch down to wait. Soon, the men and boys line up for the morning roll call. Today, the inspection is different. There are more soldiers standing around. The one who took my money is reading out names, but today it is not one long drone. Today, the names are cut with hate. The men who have been checked are being made to squat in front of the school building with their hands on their heads. The thanedaar is wearing his uniform, even his cap. The call goes on until all the men are sitting. The soldier nods his head at the thanedaar: everything is in order. They did not call out Deva's name. He is nowhere to be seen. He is no longer here. No one in this camp will ever see him again.

I start back towards the tent. There is a tussle in my chest, a beast bucking. I don't know where I find the strength, but I run. The beast is gnawing into my sides. I run past the school building, the half-dug trench and the massive sal tree. My knees feel like they will shatter but I run. I can see the tarpaulin now, the tent is weaving into my sight. When Sani gets the news, I have to be close enough to look into her eyes and hear her scream.

The sun is at its highest point. I lie down and set my head against the ground. In spite of everything that the earth has suffered, she shows her grace. She has yielded a hollow that is just right for my curved back. There is no one here at this hour. My arm is pressed against my ear but I can still hear my breath crackle like cinders. Under the edge of the tarpaulin, I can see the legs of a goat, perfectly still. I tuck my bundle under my neck and lay my arm across my tired body. The tarpaulin puffs and sighs and settles down. I am going to lie here until I hear the drummers play again.

THE AGONY OF LEAVES

I do not want to beat about this bush or that bush. I will say it straight: I am not a perverted fellow. It has never been my habit to move with prostitutes or other women of that type. Not even once have I made a lewd remark to a lady or suggested some dubious act to anyone other than my wife. I was always faithful to Lata and she will certainly vouch for that, wherever she is resting now. I am from a decent family; I have a good position in the community; I have clean hands.

Unfortunately for me, I am in love with my daughter-in-law.

And without a doubt, it is love. It is necessary to say this to challenge the obvious conclusion, that my predicament is a matter of lust and libido. The problem is society, which over and above everything else has a filthy mind. People will say: look at the dirty bugger, he has no shame, how could he even think such a thing? What I would say in response is this: look at my track record and my intentions, look at my character. After such an examination, only a clean chit can be the result. But it is my bad luck that things are not so simple.

Every morning, Meera and I sit on the veranda with our coffee, just like Lata and I did the time we went to Kodaikanal. Meera scans the paper and I scan her, although not in a way that would make her feel uncomfortable. My son Vikram usually sleeps till late so it is just the two of us, apart from Venu running back and forth from the kitchen. That boy never walks.

There is an old woman who occasionally comes in to scrub and sweep, but God only knows what she really does when she is here. Venu does most of the cooking. Meera is not the domestic type but that is not a problem because she has never had the need; nor will there ever be a need, I am sure.

Meera rustles the paper and reads out some interesting titbit: 'Principal absconds with student and college cook.'

Then she gives me a half smile and shakes her head in that special way: what will people do next? The smile that also means: what will we do next?

Long after our second cup, when the paper has slid on to the floor and Venu has trotted off into the kitchen garden, we continue to sit here, staring at the slopes. There is no need for this type of attendance on her part or on mine but we do it anyway, feeling something between thrill and anxiety.

'I really need to have my bath and start the day,' she often says, not moving.

'The day is not going anywhere,' I say.

In a few weeks, the rains will be here and the water will smash against every side of the bungalow. I suppose then we will have to go back inside. But I am not going to think about that; at the moment the sunshine is still lighting up the hillsides, every tea bush aching with green.

I have said that my feelings are not based on lust, and I maintain that position. But it has to be said that Meera is beautiful. At times, when she is lost in her own world, her face reminds me of one of those fifties tragedy queens. The expression is a little sulky; the determined chin is lowered; that loose strand is tucked behind her ear. Then our eyes will meet, I will say something about Venu or the constant damn mist up here and her spirit returns, the laughter springing out of her eyes. This week her nail polish has been chipped: it makes her look a little bold, a little mischievous. I can imagine her hands pinning my wrists down as her hair falls over my face.

Three or four tiles have fallen off the roof. Early in the day, all the taps splutter mindlessly and then spew out a muddy trickle. Somewhere there is a leak and the drip goes on through the night. I am not going to mention these things to Vikram again as it will only annoy him.

All over the house there are items that seem to have been left behind by previous occupants. There is a broken pram in the storeroom off the kitchen. A framed painting of a woman nuzzling a deer gathers cobwebs on the top shelf in my room. They are using a cricket bat as a doorstop.

And there is the smell of tea always. There are packets of dust stacked up in the storeroom. Export-quality cartons fall out of the kitchen cupboard. Cloth bags full of leaves sit in a basket on the dresser and there is more tea in its drawers. The smell is like burnt bread or sawdust or damp wood. I can't stand the stuff.

My home in Coimbatore was very different. Smaller of course, but neater. I sold it two years ago and came to live here. Vikram got a tip that a chemical plant had been given permission to set up just five kilometres away from my neighbourhood. He strongly advised me to sell the place before the property prices crashed. I can't blame him for wanting to safeguard his inheritance. So I sold it, put the money in a fixed deposit, and now I'm cooling my heels here in tea country.

Vikram has been the manager of the tea estate for nearly three years. He is hardly at home and spends most of his time 'whipping the place into shape', as he likes to announce to any visitor. According to him, the pluckers are lazy, the field supervisors are cheats and the fuel suppliers are racketeers. He explains these things to me as if I am under the impression that running an enterprise is like playing a game of gully cricket.

'We could be affected by a political crisis on the other side of the world, by fashions in Japan, incomes in Russia. You really have to keep your eye on the ball in this game,' he said a few mornings ago.

'When Russians become rich, I am sure the first thing they dream of is a hot cup of Nilgiri chai,' I said.

'Really? And when you were at the bank, rubber-stamping some clerk's thirty-thousand-rupee loan to finance his daughter's wedding, what international considerations were going through your mind then?'

'Vikram, please,' said Meera.

He shrugged and walked out onto the veranda, yelling for one of the workers.

The estate is owned by the Sisodias and they are the centre of our universe here, even though sometimes they are not seen for months. Old Man Sisodia, what more can be said about him? I think even God is afraid to tell him his innings are nearly over. The elder Sisodia son concerns himself with other aspects of their businesses: the plastics and the cement. The younger Sisodia son is in charge of the sugar and tea. I mentioned that he just needs to buy a dairy farm and then he will be all set, but Vikram did not even smile. That boy thinks the Sisodias are gods.

There is also a Sisodia nephew and he is the one that we see the most. He comes here in his jeep, wearing sunglasses even when the afternoon is thick with fog.

When he is around, we see even less of Vikram. They say they are going to Coonoor for meetings and auctions and then do not return for a few days. They play golf. They go horse riding. I am sure Vikram will have said that he has ridden ever since he can remember. I have learnt that there are many things about his past that have been adjusted for the benefit of the Sisodia family.

A few nights ago, I lay in bed listening to that damn drip. I thought a slow count during the interval between each drop would send me to sleep. But it only made me more restless. I found myself becoming anxious if the drop did not arrive on time. So I got up to go to the bathroom. In the corridor, I could see a rectangle of light coming from their room. I walked to the edge of the door. In the gap between the hinges, I saw what Vikram hides from the world.

He was asleep on the bedspread, his shirt still tucked into his trousers, the sound of his snores rasping and angry. Meera was sitting up on her side, her head leaning back against the wall. There was a book open in her lap, but her eyes were closed. Her plait hung down one side, stopping at the place where the buttons on her nightie began. This was not a woman asleep; this was a woman in suspense.

I have been a husband. I know that there are secrets from the world, other lives in the darkness. But Meera is an exceptional woman and does not deserve to be treated in this shabby way. Look at you, Vikram, I thought; look at this tip-top man. A man who comes home too drunk even to talk to the woman who has spent the day sitting on the veranda, wondering what her life would have been like in a place far away from this wilderness. Meera's head did not nod or drop as I watched. That is how I know she was awake. I think she sensed my presence and yet she did not move. She left the door ajar and the light on for me, in defiance of her husband's sour breaths.

I withdrew. In the bathroom, I looked at my face, sitting solidly above my too-big pyjamas. A man my age must be allowed to have a last frolic in his head. Allow me, Meera, I said to myself: whom does it hurt? It is not as if anything will actually happen.

Not all happiness has to be big. Lata knew that, and I have no doubt that it was a certainty she had even before we were married. I turned down promotion after promotion because I did not want to be transferred to some godforsaken place every few years. I did not want to be involved with the politics of the managers. I did what I was asked, and that was enough. It did not diminish us.

When Lata and I went to Kodaikanal, on the final day we decided to have coffee at a posh hotel. There was no one sitting at the table next to us; only a dog asleep on a chair. About a half dozen silver bowls were spread across the white tablecloth, some nearly full of a creamy dessert, ordered but not eaten. Various hotel staff members were loafing near the restaurant door but we were simply left to sit there for a long time. We did not mind as it gave us ample opportunity to take in the surroundings: the huge windows looking out on to the lawn, the yards of red velvet, the fireplace.

A bearer finally came to take our order, wearing a turban that looked like a giant bird was seated on his head. As he turned away from us, a woman came into the restaurant to retrieve the dog. Her hair was piled up in a strange sculpture and she wore a furry black jacket.

'Chikita,' she said.

The way she swung her large hips reminded me of the gait of a boar.

'Chiki-liki-tiki-ta.'

The dog sprang off the chair and they left the restaurant together: the dog and the boar.

When it came, the coffee was expensive, lukewarm and tasteless. Barely able to hide our giggles, Lata and I left the restaurant. We were just like little children. And we strolled back down to the lake, as if we were the only people in the place who knew a precious secret.

So that is what we were. Dinner dances were for people in films. The first time I tasted beer, I was in my forties. The only people in our lives were our relations and neighbours. In our house there was some coming and going, there were festivals, I thought there was fun. But all this holds no value for Vikram. All he can see is that I shared the same desk at the same bank for twenty years, and that one night at his club I mixed up Canada and Canberra.

To get to this estate you have to leave Coonoor on NH67, the road to Mettupalayam, and take a left after the sign for the army memorial. Then, just past the Lakshmi Devi Women's Cooperative building, there is a side road, too narrow for two vehicles to pass each other. The road rises through a stretch of silver oak and eucalyptus trees. After a couple of kilometres, there is a board indicating the road to the Greencrest Tea Estate. The planters who live at the estate are our nearest neighbours, a most dismal couple that Vikram seeks out when he is particularly bored. The man mumbles and looks like he wears face powder; the woman flashes large yellowing teeth when she laughs and is always spilling food on herself. After the Greencrest turning, the road narrows further and continues for another six or seven kilometres before stopping at our high metal gate.

Meera and I have been playing rummy all afternoon. I am not really fond of the game. But we can prolong our chat around the routine of the cards. I am wearing my maroon sweater, the stylish one.

'It looks like it's getting clear outside,' says Meera. 'Shall we take a small walk?'

'No, I think better to leave it for today. I still feel a bit of heaviness in my chest.'

'Maybe tomorrow then. Here, show.'

She drops a card and then splays the rest out, her elegant fingers resting between us on the sofa.

'I think you were just trying to distract me with all your chattering about walks. Points on this game to be discounted.'

'You are the chattering one, Appa. Not only will we count the points, we'll double them as a penalty for your attempted cheating.'

'Who do you think you're calling a cheater?'

She laughs and begins to gather up the cards.

I clasp her hand to stop her. Our hands are locked, my palm covering her knuckles, warmth passing between us. My fingers curl up and press into her buttery skin. I run my thumb up her little finger in the most natural way.

She stands up and the cards fall from her lap. I try to grab her hand again, but she shakes me off. Even though my heart is racing, I take comfort from the fact that she does not look angry. Hers is not a face of disgust or shame or fury. It is something else entirely that I cannot place.

'Venu,' she calls, heading to the kitchen. 'Venu.'

I pick up the fallen cards one by one, peeling them off the floor. I look at the two faces on the jack of clubs. They look back at me.

Vikram seems to be in an unusually good mood tonight. That leads me to believe that Meera has not said anything to him. They are going to the club to meet a German tea taster, some sort of world champion in the business.

'You know, Appa, it is such a bloody pleasure to meet someone who really knows what he is talking about, especially when you share the same passions,' says Vikram, knotting his tie.

I don't know what passions he is talking about, but I assume it is tea since that is what this poor German spends his life tasting. As far as I know, Vikram never gave two damns about tea. I still don't think he does. If the Sisodias offered him a more senior position in an insurance company or a car business, he would run there before the words had even fully left their mouths. But this poor German will never know that.

'I met Jürgen and his wife at the Sisodias' place in London,' says Vikram. 'Lovely couple.'

Meera has not said one word since she came out of the room, dressed for their dinner. She is wearing a pink sari with a silver border and her hair is up, making her neck look long and regal. While Vikram is fussing with his shoelaces, she walks over to the window. The night is completely black already and Venu has switched on the veranda lights. Her blouse is cut low at the back: its arc is making my head spin. There are about two handspans of skin above the fastening, a complicated knot with silver tassels.

I am now sure that she has not mentioned anything to Vikram. She has decided to let it pass, a malfunction in her father-in-law's head, momentary and not serious. Maybe she did not even recognize it as irregular. These things happen: a brush or a knock or a bump.

The scent she uses for special occasions is in the air.

'His English is excellent,' says Vikram, smiling at Meera's back. 'He certainly knows all the lingo.'

She does not turn around.

These tea fellows think they have invented a language. They like to explain to the layman the meaning of a 'second flush'; how the product can become 'chesty' when it is tainted with the smell of packing materials; that when boiling water is poured over tea, the agitation in the cup is 'the agony of leaves'. To make sure you understand, they tell you twice, and then a third time.

'Darling, shall we go?'

Vikram is ready. Meera nods and walks towards the door. My head is filling with blood. She will not leave without wishing me a good night, without giving me some indication.

'Appa, we will see you in the morning. If you need some coffee or something, can you wake Venu and ask him to do it? You know what happened last time,' says Vikram.

She is adjusting her shawl in the doorway. I stand up and take a step forward. It will remind her that I am here, that all I need is one look.

'And don't touch the bolts. We will lock it from the outside.'

She is now standing by the balustrade. I stop myself calling out.

Vikram pats his jacket pockets and steps outside. The door swings shut and I hear her heels move away on the veranda boards.

Lata went through a bad time after her mother died. Only now do I realize how bad it was. One night, I returned to our house and not a single light was on. It was all the more mystifying because it was the day before Deepavali. Ours was the only house on the street looking like that, a hole where a home should have been.

Inside, there was more darkness. Vikram was at a neighbour's house. Lata was lying on our bed, her arms crossed over her face. I shook her shoulder.

'I'm awake,' she said.

'Are you sick?'

I could barely hear my voice over the sound of the fireworks rattling and cracking up and down the street.

'I can't get up,' she said.

I thought she meant that there was something wrong with her back or her legs. I asked her if she needed to go to the hospital.

'I have been trying for months but I just can't get up,' she said.

It was then that I understood.

'You must not be weak,' I said. 'You must be strong.'

She reached out and took my hand with a force I had not felt before. She held it in that strange spinning light and we stayed that way for most of the night, watching the colours rocket past the window.

Here, at night in the Nilgiri Hills, there is no light, no noise. This is a place where dogs don't howl, babies don't cry, people don't speak. Out on the terraces, I have noticed that under every shrub there exists a different kind of silence.

'Where is Meera?' I ask Venu the next morning.

'They came in very late. Madam said she has a headache. She's sleeping.'

I continue with my brain-teaser game. It involves balls placed in a series of boxes. The aim is to identify the number and colour of the balls in each box but I can't even work out how many colours there are supposed to be. I give up.

It has started to rain. Not the forceful storms that we expected, but something meagre and gasping. The slopes have lost all colour. Today, they are only slabs of charcoal, ready to slide down towards the wet plains.

Venu has a cough: an uneven, high-pitched, bouncing affliction. Apart from the whooshing of the drizzle, it is the only sound in the bungalow.

Meera does not leave her room all day.

The TV screen here only features a range of shades from blue to grey. I have been informed that it is something to do with the altitude and the way the cables are laid, but I have not attempted to understand this reasoning. So whether it is an evening serial or the news or a music programme, the participants always look depressed or terminally ill.

Meera continues to avoid me. There can be no doubt that my foolish action has scared and upset her. I have to make things as they were, no matter what it takes. There is no other way for us to live here. I will beg her for forgiveness and she will take pity on me. Vikram will never have to know about any of this.

I am a fool: a detestable old fool.

Meera is nowhere to be seen. I was on my own at breakfast, with Venu being excessively polite, as if he was mocking my presence. According to him, a friend came to pick her up but I am sure this is a tall tale. I have been on the lookout since early morning, and I did not hear any car outside.

I go into their room and look around: there are no clues. Her brown handbag is on the dressing table but she could have taken a different one, I suppose. I open the wardrobe door and stare at the jumble of shoes. I crouch down and pick up a high heel – a silky bow dangles off its strap. Where exactly on her leg would that bow be positioned? Around the ankle or perhaps higher up somewhere. I pick at the bow, working at the knot with both hands, plucking and pulling, but it won't come undone. With my nails I burrow into the fabric. I tear at it with my teeth, sputtering out the glossy fibres that stick to my tongue. It seems ridiculous that I cannot do anything with this knot. In the end, I exhaust myself and drop the shoe back into the wardrobe.

I hear the sound of a blade hitting a board in the kitchen, and I follow it because I can't be alone. Venu is sitting on the floor, cutting eyes out of potatoes. It only now occurs to me that he seems to be here all the time. Since I arrived he does not appear to have taken any leave, visited any family or gone off to have a good time. I want to ask him something about his life, but he gives me a look of such wariness; a look that says he is tired of living with the obscene knowledge in his possession. I turn around and leave the kitchen.

In the sitting room cabinet, there is a nearly full bottle of foreign whisky. You see that in films. The man facing a crisis strides into a room; he pulls the bottle towards him, unscrews the cap and tosses it over his shoulder; the very sound of the liquid glugging into the glass is comforting;

we know that he will soon be restored; he throws it back in one gulp; his eyes return to focus; he repeats. They don't tell you that you will get a headache even before your second sip; that its smell will make your eyes water; that what you fear will leap from your heart into your head.

'Not with soda, Appa. Never with soda. With ice, fine. If you must,' Vikram once said to me.

So, in spite of myself, I begin drinking the whisky as it is, with neither soda nor ice. It is what Vikram would want.

When Meera returns home, I am still in the sitting room.

She turns on the light and starts.

'You gave me a shock. Why are you sitting in the dark?'

These are the first words she has said to me for days.

I draw myself off the sofa, reordering the sentences that I have prepared, the thing that must be said.

As if sensing that what I am going to say will not be to her liking, she turns away.

'Wait, please wait,' I say.

Her gaze falls to the glass on the floor.

'You've been drinking?'

'I've been thinking, about you.'

'You sound strange. Are you drunk?'

'No. I am sorry.'

'What?'

I move forward but my legs are so unsteady that I drop to my knees, clutching the side of the armchair for support. I dare not look at her, so instead I look in her direction where I see a whirl of books and cushions and leather and wood and the floor. I begin to speak.

'I don't want you to misunderstand me, about what happened, which was a mistake, a misunderstanding you see, but I am very sorry, I never meant to make you angry or hurt you when you have been so kind to me, the type of kindness, I can't explain.'

'Appa, stop.'

'No, please, you need to understand because I don't think you understand my position at all.'

I stop speaking because a wave of nausea comes over me.

Her voice is a whisper: 'Don't do this. I don't know what you want from me.'

I wish she would understand that I am doing this in order to stop it; to reassure her that it will never happen again; that our lives will return to that gentle order on which we are both so dependent. She does not seem to understand so I need to make one last effort to bring clarity. I need to end the confusion.

I think of getting to my feet but instead approach her on my hands and knees, going from the softness of the carpet to the hard wooden floor where she is standing. I stretch out but slip. I am lying on the floor now, and my hands reach out and touch her ankles.

'Meera,' I say.

I look up.

In her eyes, there is the pity that comes with horror. She begins to sob, great shuddering breaths that terrify me. I lay my forehead on the ground and plead with her to listen to me. Her feet give off the chill of these hills, and I know that she will jerk them free at any moment.

I know what I am saying, but I cannot be sure if she is able to hear me. Her sobs are too loud, the lights are too bright, the hour is too late. I have to reverse the clock and I am prepared to keep explaining until I have made amends.

I begin again when there is the sound of footsteps on the veranda, snuffing out my words. The door crashes open. I turn my head and see Vikram in the doorway, his proportions all wrong, the head so far away, the torso wide, the legs endless. Through the smears of my sight I now see that he is not alone. Behind him stands the Sisodia nephew, his head to one side, as if he has averted his eyes.

Solid bands of mist have encircled the bungalow over the past few days. Yesterday, I could not even see the fence from my window. Today is not much better. The bands are the same shades of blue and grey as the TV screen.

I am trying a new brain-teaser. This one involves ordering a set of circles, each with a number in the centre, so that applying a given formula to the set yields a specific number. It is more difficult than I thought it would be.

I hear Venu's tread. It is accompanied by the trembling of a cup on a saucer. Strange that it should be so loud, this rattle, and curiously slow as if it has something to announce. Even though it is only a few paces from the kitchen to where I am sitting, the sound continues, the clattering of china. I recognize that I am expecting the cup to fall, to shatter into a thousand pieces. Then I see Venu and he puts the cup and saucer down in front of me.

'Sir had phoned,' he says. 'They are staying there a few more days. They are coming back, maybe next week, maybe later.'

'I see.'

'Sir, tea?'

I look at the steam rising from the cup on the table.

'No, not for me,' I say. 'No more tea.'

THE TROUBLE WITH DINING OUT

A stroll to the restaurant had seemed like a good idea, but it was still too humid and Roma's heels were too high. They wove through the Sunday evening crowds on the seafront, past the brass band and the balloon vendors. It was high tide and clouds of spray rose up over the sea wall. A family was having their picture taken in front of the Gandhi statue – Roma called out to Amit but he walked squarely into the shot.

As they turned into a side street, Roma glanced down: her foot looked strangled by the gold straps of her sandal, the second toe raised, as if struggling for air, the little toe pinker than usual under the slash of dark polish.

'It's only five minutes away. And no one asked you to wear those shoes,' said Amit.

'You have a big sweat patch on your back,' said Roma.

When they arrived at the restaurant, they paused in the sudden chill of the foyer, waiting for the hostess's attention.

'Does my shirt still look . . . ?' he asked.

'No,' she lied.

When the hostess turned to them, she murmured in a tone that spoke of marble, mirrors and soft leather.

Amit said to Roma: 'They are already here.'

They followed the hostess down the aisle, stepping in and out of pools of light, past a water feature and towers of orchids, to the corner table where Brij and Sabine sat like forms carved into the restaurant's dark wood panels. Behind them, a searchlight caught the shimmer of rolling waves.

'Brij,' said Amit.

'Amit,' said Brij.

'Gosh,' said Sabine.

The hostess smiled and walked away without a sound, the light catching her earrings.

Roma noted that Sabine's hair was newly bobbed and looked like it had been styled in consultation with the restaurant's architects. She wondered how long it would be before Paris was mentioned. Sabine had a French grandparent, long dead, who was invoked whenever possible. Formerly called Sabina, she had snipped off the last syllable. And even though she spoke little French, the words she knew she pronounced with a histrionic correctness.

'Roma,' said Brij.

He leaned in to kiss her, smiling like a man who turned on his good humour with a tap on a touchscreen. Roma felt his hand slide down her back, his thumb lingering and pressing into her spine. She drew back and her hip knocked against the table. A glass shook. She looked to see if Amit or Sabine had noticed, but they were trying to recall when they had last seen each other.

'I give up, it's too difficult,' said Sabine, leaning back in her seat.

'I have already ordered the wine. It's a goodie. Hope that's okay,' said Brij.

'Absolutely fine. You're the man for that,' said Amit.

Roma put her clutch down on a corner of the table and shifted in her seat. Brij was looking at her breasts. There was no suggestion of a glimpse or a peek; his was a studied appraisal, a tour of the flesh below her collarbone, the dip of her neckline and the swell of her blouse. She cast her eyes downwards to see if she had any cleavage showing, whether fabric had ridden down or a seam slipped. He caught the look and acknowledged it as a sign of consensus.

Roma looked again at Amit, but he appeared oblivious. Conscious of Brij's numerous trusteeships and directorships, he was talking about the difficulties in getting a position as an orthopaedic consultant in the premier hospitals.

He mentioned a trauma symposium he was to attend in Edinburgh and the tightness of his schedule. He said that it was great to be so busy. He shrugged, smiled and shifted his chopsticks about on the table.

It was obvious to Roma that Brij was not listening to a word Amit said of his work conditions or his plans for advancement. She too had stopped listening – all she could focus on was the sight of Brij's fingers stroking the surface of the tablecloth, running lazy loops from his glass to the edge of the table.

Sabine said that the previous night had stretched into the early hours and they were feeling the effects: drinks and dinner with a friend who was a curator at the Musée d'Orsay.

'Speak for yourself,' said Brij. 'I'm absolutely fine.'

'He was telling us about a recent acquisition they have made, a stunning mahogany art deco dressing table. The way dear Eustache describes these treasures, he really makes them come alive. But such a tragedy, the original mirror broke in transit and will have to be replaced. Of course, it was insured and blah blah blah, but that's it, the piece will never be the same again,' said Sabine.

The waiter placed a bowl before Roma. Pieces of conger eel glistened in their broth, its surface flecked with yellow chrysanthemum petals. The steam smelt of the dark rock pools that appeared on the shore when the tide drew out.

'Looks delicious,' said Brij to Roma.

'This is all so light and lovely, doesn't at all upset the regime,' said Sabine with a profoundly guttural 'r'.

Brij reached for the bottle of wine and motioned towards Roma's half-full glass.

'No thanks, I'm fine for now,' she said.

He poured anyway, to about an inch from the top, looking at her the whole time. Sabine put down her chopsticks. Amit picked his up.

'Coming back to what we were saying,' said Sabine, 'I think it's too fussy, too loud and showy. Whose benefit is all this for? I don't understand why the organizers can't show a little, I don't know, restraint.'

'Absolutely,' said Amit.

Roma braved a glance at Brij. There were plenty of women – and men too, she supposed – who would find him handsome, dashing even. He had fleshy lips that seemed to move even when he was not talking or eating. His hair was slightly longer than it ought to be, curling up over his collar, a mark of some imagined iconoclasm. He looked like he had shaved recently, his jaw appearing almost laundered. She imagined his bathroom cabinet: a deadly blade lodged in an old-fashioned razor; a tortoiseshell comb with sharp teeth; cubes of odourless soaps; aftershave lotions that burned on impact.

'The hyoid bone is here, quite high up in the throat area. I don't see how he can have broken that while dancing,' said Amit.

'I didn't say he was a good dancer,' said Sabine.

Brij leaned back in his chair and looked at Roma again. He picked up his glass and took a large sip.

Roma ran her finger over the smooth surface of the chopstick rest. It could have been a fossil, a product of the world tamping down its past, layers of urushi and pine needles and seashell and gold leaf coalescing into this precise element of tableware. She closed her fist around it and let it grow hot in her hand.

A waiter placed a bloom of pufferfish sashimi on the table, served with a thimble of ponzu sauce, the slices cut so thin that they looked like they would pop when pierced.

'Sarita's delightful when she needs a favour but the rest of the time she's an absolute seven-star witch. You know, she has a PA now? How much organization can it take to show up at the gym by three in the afternoon? Oh but I forget, she had that job as creative muse for that oaf in Dubai. Although that was a while ago. Anyway, this PA, God only knows where Sarita fished her out from,' said Sabine.

Roma's skin felt raw from having been out in the sun. Earlier in the day, as Amit dozed on the balcony, she had slipped out of the hotel room and taken a taxi to a nearby beach. But it was the wrong beach. There was a smell of dried fish in the air, crows pecked at rotting fruit, and a wave left a plastic bag wrapped around her foot. Then she had seen a dead turtle beached on the sand.

Sabine had turned to the subject of Brij's brother who was in the middle of a divorce in New York.

'So, first his wife tried to hack his emails, of course with no success since she lacks any kind of expertise, technical or otherwise. Then she went out and bought an audio surveillance transmitter to listen to the conversations he had in his car. It just wouldn't be believable, even in some awful airport novel,' said Sabine.

'Isn't that illegal wiretapping?' asked Amit.

'Of course it is, but Brij's sister-in-law wouldn't let something as trivial as legality get in the way of her personality disorders.'

'This can't be true.'

'There's so much more I could tell you. He decided not to go to the police for the sake of the children.'

'What could have got into her?'

'She actually said that she didn't understand what all the fuss was about, that if he had nothing to hide, he wouldn't care whether anyone listened to his conversations or not.'

'She just cracked, I suppose,' said Brij. After a pause: 'What do you think, Roma?'

'But can you understand what they are actually doing on stage?' asked Amit.

'You have to place it in context,' said Sabine.

'In the context of what?'

'Of what they are trying to achieve. It's not really a performance, more of a slow descent into a primal state.'

'I see.'

She was convinced now that Amit was only pretending not to notice, that it was convenient and comfortable for him not to react. There was a teardrop of dry skin just below his right ear, red and peeling. She recalled her insistence the day before that they should cancel the dinner. They were on holiday and a chance meeting with Brij and Sabine did not have to turn into an elaborate night out, hours of protocol and performance. But Amit had chipped away at her resistance that night and the next morning.

'At least come for the food. It's an award-winning restaurant – we're lucky it's arrived in India. And in Pondicherry, of all places.'

She thought of her flair for capitulation, the pride that she believed could no longer be injured, the daily increase in her lassitude; she thought of the long evenings she had spent providing Amit with encouragement and reassurance; she thought of the praise she had lavished and the counsel she had kept; she thought of the bags meticulously packed, the dinner parties organized, the family members appeased; she thought of the husbandry, the administration, the sex. She had faced the hot fear that nothing would ever be enough for her, and she had resisted it.

And she thought that if she looked across the table now, Brij would be smirking at her with the decisive carnality of someone who had never suffered a snub.

'I love the delicacy of Swiss villages,' said Sabine. 'They look like a flick of the wrist would make them tumble down the valley.'

Roma tilted her glass, the surface of the water forming a deep slant. It was not as if there had never been temptation or opportunity. There had been men, at least two, who had thrilled and disturbed her, men who had promised to gild her with exhilaration, one whose throwaway utterances she had studied like coded messages, and another whose wife she had been forced to let go as a friend in order to avoid seeing him.

She glanced at Amit. His back looked hunched, his voice sounded craven, his conversation was wretched when it was not asinine. She realized that over the years a hard, contemptuous thing had trailed her, like an object attached to her hem. It had witnessed the anniversary dinners, the surprise bottles of perfume, the weekend trips with other couples. And it had ended up here, coiled in a corner of the restaurant, scene of Amit's deliberate blindness to the grim seduction being played out in front of him.

The waiter set down the tempura of silver sillago and angelica tree buds, piled on the dish like a heap of severed claws.

'I saw a dead turtle on the beach today,' said Roma.

But they were all laughing at Brij's joke and did not hear her.

If she sedated herself, dulled all her responses, neutralized anything that fell within the realm of disgust or outrage, she could see herself walking into a hotel suite with Brij. The set of rooms he always took, with the flowers as they should be, the corner lamps lit in the middle of the afternoon, a view of the sea. He would be impatient, proceedings would begin seconds after the key card was slipped into its slot and the door kicked shut. She would try to identify the taste in his mouth, the maltiness of beer, the freshness of aniseed. There might be a brief interlude as drinks were poured, not a concession to romance but a mechanical imperative: fuel or lubrication. The champagne would foam over his wrists and leave a wet trail on the thick pile. She imagined that he would want to touch her cheek, drag his chin down its length so that she could feel the graze of his stubble before his fingers pressed into the base of her neck.

'Excuse me for just a moment,' said Roma, tossing her napkin on to the table. Picking up her clutch, she turned to go to the ladies', aware that the conversation would falter the moment her back was turned, that Brij and Sabine would watch her walk across the restaurant, see the light catch the span of silk at her waist, read the motion of her shoulders, sense the heat from her skin.

She pushed open the heavy wooden door and put her bag down on the marble top. She applied a little powder over her face to temper the flush, put some hydrating drops into her eyes and touched up her lipstick. She re-pinned her pallu to reveal a little more above her neckline. Then she made her way back to the table, head lowered, the gait of the desirable, conceding the inevitability of the room's gaze, allowing it as part of a social pact. It was only temporary; she knew that all too well. In time, a new bargain would have to be made with her body.

A glass partition ran along one side of the passage, a sheet that appeared to have trapped within it chunks of melting ice, wisps of smoke, crystals and gems. Through the glass she could make out the shape of their table, the hazy sheen of Sabine's hair, the movement of Amit's gesturing hands, Brij's solid mass.

'What did I miss?' she asked, sitting down, smoothing the stiff cotton of the napkin over her lap and then looking directly at Brij.

Sake had arrived in her absence, and she let it burn its way down her throat.

'Brij was telling us about Africa,' said Amit.

'Tell me about Africa,' said Roma to Brij.

'I would love to tell you about Africa.'

'Any particular part of it?'

'Mozambique.'

'Mozambique.'

'Massive coal reserves. We have just started something there now. They are bending over backwards, rolling out every red carpet. It's really something to see.'

'I'm sure it is. So what else are you doing?'

'We are looking at Liberia too.'

'And how does Liberia look?'

'Pretty damn promising at the moment. Gold, diamonds, iron ore. There's huge potential there. We have some contacts in Monrovia, so hopefully things will move fast. There's definitely a new scramble on.' Brij laughed.

Sabine looked tired now. Every few minutes, she closed her eyes for a couple of seconds as if she was trying to instigate a revival. One of her hands moved with a slight tremor. Her neck looked thin and frail. It would not be able to bear the weight of her head for much longer, the tissue would fall away, the tendons would strain and snap. The lights on the promenade behind were strung out in a sequence of white, gold and amber until they stopped dead at the blackness of the sea.

'Can you remember their names, the people we met at Victor's?' asked Amit.

Roma ignored him, not even bothering with a shrug or a nod. It was as if he had said nothing at all. She kept her eyes on Brij, her expression flickering at the edges of amusement and enquiry. He looked like he was toying with the inevitable outcome of his desire, tossing it from one hand to the other, already on the verge of becoming bored with it.

The hostess returned to ask how they were enjoying their evening, and made a minute adjustment to one of the fleshy stems in the table centrepiece.

Amit began an account, who knew whether true or false, from his time in medical college, a time of high jinks, when his spirit of adventure involved him in fiendish capers, when he and his close-knit group of friends entertained and bewitched in equal measure. Roma's mind drifted to the walk back to their hotel, the silence in the room as they got ready for bed. She saw the web of hairs that fanned out from Amit's navel, glistening over his nascent paunch, a place that he scratched often as he slept. She made a knot in the napkin on her lap, and then another, and one more, until it was a gnarled ball that she could let drop on to the floor. It landed in the middle of the aisle, unseen by the others.

Roma continued to fix her gaze on Brij. She made sure he was not listening to Amit, locking her hands loosely on the table, parting her lips, leaving a space that would only just accommodate the tip of an index finger.

'Crazy days,' said Amit.

'But long gone,' said Sabine, 'and now what?'

'We have a bright future,' said Brij.

He ordered another bottle of wine and nodded at an acquaintance at another table. Then he turned back to Roma.

'Would you like me to tell you what the future holds?' she asked.

'Please do.'

'You'll have to give me your hand.'

'My hand?'

'The future is written on your palm.'

'I see, you're a palmist, are you?'

'I am.'

Amit was immobile; Roma could see his unchanged profile.

She took Brij's hand. His fingers were long and thick and seemed full of a latent energy, intending at any moment to try and escape her clasp. If there was anything to be done, they would do it. She ran a nail over a deep-set groove on his palm.

'This, you see, is the life line.'

'I see.'

'You seem to have been blessed with an endless one.'

'Really?'

'It looks like it goes halfway up your wrist.'

'If you say so, Roma.'

She pulled his hand closer and undid the clasp of his cufflink. She lifted the onyx panther head clear of the buttonhole and dropped the cufflink onto the table. Slowly and precisely, she folded his cuff back up along his arm until it formed a neat band under his elbow. His forearm was pale, firm, a thick vein forking its way towards his palm. She ran her fingers down his arm, her thumb settling on his wrist.

'Look at that,' she said. 'The line stops here. This is where it ends.'

She could feel his pulse, a great clap that was like the sound of something approaching, a beat that matched the rhythm of the trembling walls, the seesawing ceiling, the night sky of Pondicherry rotating over the sea.

She gripped Brij's hand hard and lifted her head to look at Amit. He was gazing at the cufflink, his features showing only a sad harmlessness.

She leaned forward, the edge of the table digging into her stomach.

Sabine was sliding a scallop around on her plate: shifting, propelling but not eating.

Brij took back his hand and raised his glass.

'Cheers, Roma,' he said.

Amit looked at Sabine's bowed head and then back at his lap before letting out a delicate cough.

Two waiters hurried past their table towards the water feature that had begun to spurt ungainly jets over the stone rim and onto the parquet. Another waiter was laying down towels as a fourth struggled with the tap at the base of the wall. A momentary hush descended on the restaurant and it seemed to Roma like the most human reverberation she had ever heard. Sabine's eyes were closed, Brij was putting his cufflink back on, Amit's hands lay flat in his lap. Behind them, a thin runnel was inching down the aisle between two sets of tables. The hostess gestured to the waiter with a finger, avoided the splash with an elegant hop and walked back towards her station.

GOLDEN LADDER

It took about thirty hours to get from Ithaca to Udaipur. Falguni had done the best that she could on each flight along the way, flicking through indistinguishable comedies and forcing herself to read articles on surf schools and organic vineyards. She had tried to nibble at the beige offerings in their plastic trays. Occasionally, she had closed her eyes, hoping to doze.

She emerged from the terminal building on time, but the car that would take her on to Neelgarh was late. It could genuinely have had engine trouble; or, more likely, the delay was the first stage in her uncle's reassertion of his writ. She bought a cup of tea and drank it, perched on her suitcase, absently watching the desperate smokers who dropped everything to light up the moment they came through the sliding doors. She was asked in English if she wanted a taxi or accommodation, and one man in a red kurta asked her what her name was. She ignored them all.

For her journey she was wearing a belted smock, its line marred by the paperback in its right pocket. Her fringe was stealing towards the top of her glasses and the cranberry lip balm had glazed and gummed her mouth. In Ithaca, she wore scratchy woollen shift dresses in grey or navy for winter, and men's shirts with the top button fastened in the summer. Her workman boots remained the same. But in spite of this uniform, there remained one vestige of her life in the family haveli: an amulet that hung around her neck on a leather cord. Tucked under her layers of clothing, a battered disc bore the form of the family god, identifiable by the symmetry of its four silver arms.

Falguni wove around trolleys and cases towards a free bench she had spotted. She picked up the film magazine left on the seat and creased it into a tight roll. Sitting down, she beat time against her knees with her makeshift baton.

Her uncle had called her two days ago, as she returned to her apartment in the darkness of a December afternoon.

'I wanted to speak to you before you hear from anyone else or see something in the news,' said his faint voice.

'What's happened, Chachaji?'

'You shouldn't worry. None of us know how they got there, someone may have planted them, people are definitely making mischief.'

'I don't understand. What's happened?'

'But we are all fine and there is nothing to worry about, that is the main thing.'

'I'm sorry, Chachaji, but what are you talking about?'

'On the property, they have found something.'

'What?'

'They are calling it a mass grave.'

The closest she had come to such a crime was the documentary shot by a colleague recently returned from a research trip to East Timor. In the course of an interview, a Timorese scholar had paused, trying to find the appropriate language.

'We have to be careful when we go into the forests, disturbing what appears to be settled, preparing ourselves for the worst,' she had said. 'Decades of brutality have been buried there, waiting to be uncovered.'

The woman's face had filled the frame, its expression a sign of quiet fatigue.

Now, the same lexicon had found its way into Falguni's family, leading her back to Neelgarh, the familiar resignation replaced by a dread stretched taut over her breast.

'Can you please turn the AC down?' Falguni asked the driver.

'You're feeling the cold here? I thought you just came from winter in America,' said her uncle, Veerendra.

Their jeep was flagged through a police checkpoint but then there were a series of delays. A group of women got off a bus in the middle of a junction and had to have their luggage thrown down to them from the roof rack. A little further on, a truck spilling sugar cane halted in the road, its driver suffering a torrent of abuse. At the railway crossing, Falguni watched as men on motorbikes blinked at their reflections in the vehicle's blacked-out windows.

'How long have they been there?' she asked, turning to Veerendra.

'Who?'

'The bodies. I don't know what to call them. The bones.'

'You can call them whatever you want. Bones, remains, dust. It makes no difference to these people: the press, the activists. What they want is our blood, I tell you. It has nothing to do with what has been found.'

'But what have the police said? Who are they?'

'Who *were* they.'

'Who were they?'

'How should I know? How would any of us know? Thousands of hectares of land and we are supposed to be responsible for every leaf, every stone that ends up there. Yes, I am sure whatever happened to them should not have happened, but why are they trying to connect us to some inexplicable thing that happened in another age?'

'How can you say things like that?'

Veerendra spoke in a voice accustomed to being heeded.

'Things like what? Are they the first mysterious deaths in this country? Will they be the last? Let the police or whoever make their investigations and do what they have to do. We are not stopping them. But talking nonsense about atrocities and vendettas and such things. The bastards have not even confirmed where the bodies came from.'

The car swerved to avoid a pothole, and when Falguni lurched against the window, Veerendra looked as though he was enjoying her discomfort. The figures of Krishna and Radha, hanging from the rear-view mirror, flailed violently on their string.

'We know nothing about these people. How will they be identified after all this time? We don't have records and lists like your America,' he continued.

The car left the highway and turned eastwards, watched by a vulture at the top of a tree. Pairs of oxen lined the road that led into the belly of the Chauhan lands, a place of fragile saplings and timid temple domes, occasionally thrown into disarray by a cruel dust storm.

'I know what you are like,' Veerendra continued. 'Say what you like in here and finish it off. Everyone in the haveli is upset enough as it is. You don't have to make everything worse for them when you arrive.'

'There's still an hour of driving to go. Plenty of time for me to finish it off, na?'

Veerendra indicated the driver with his chin and shot her a look of disdain.

The car raced past a village primary school, its walls bleached to a sad pink. A flagless pole was planted in the hard earth in front of the building. The gate was fastened with a huge rusting padlock.

The silence between them cooled and thickened until her uncle cleared his throat, a gesture of finality.

'Your mother is the one who has been asking for you to come,' he said. 'I'm not sure why.'

The Chauhans of Neelgarh liked to talk about their distant past: how they emerged from the fist of the fire god and appeared on this land. Fierce warriors, they advanced across the spine of the Aravallis, crossed the Sabarmati, its waters red with the blood of their battles, and claimed the low hills in the distance.

Since anyone could remember, their status had been beyond dispute but not beyond discussion. In tea shops, villagers would reflect on the family's proximity to the power brokers of Delhi; in the bazaar, the haveli cooks would boast about the vast quantities of saffron used in the kitchen every month. When a new temple was built in Neelgarh, a statue of one of the most prominent Chauhans also went up in front of the primary school.

But chinks were beginning to show in the devotion that the family had always seen as their due. New alliances were forming far from the ancestral seat, different friendships warming over the brazier of patronage. The most recent parliament was the first time since independence that a Neelgarh Chauhan was not returned to his rightful seat in the Lok Sabha.

The grand piano in the haveli's ballroom, imported from Austria over fifty years ago, now covered with a yellowing sheet; the teak chests full of moths; the stone fish in the fountain speckled green by the years; the cracked flagstones in the courtyards; the lantern, opaque with soot, swinging slowly in a turret: they all spoke of a cold, irrevocable fate.

The family, however, was convinced of its power to preserve this known world for posterity. The haveli was made of marble, not wattle. Even the most inauspicious of days eventually came to an end. The Chauhans' strength, they believed, flowed from the laws of gods, before which the laws of men would scatter like chaff in the wind.

Even as far as Sirohi, the jeep was recognized. Outside a tea stall, two labourers knocked over a stool in their haste to stand up. On the veranda of a dispensary, a policeman put his hands together. Salaams rained down from the newly constructed overpass, a consequence of calibrated Chauhan generosity. The jeep shot through the hamlets, its windows revealing nothing.

Falguni kept her eyes on the dancing figures of Krishna and Radha. Veerendra's fingers drummed happily on the seat, as if denying the recent conversation and the presence of human remains on the lands he gazed at every morning.

'I suppose we should be grateful that they are not out making a spectacle on the streets today. Whoever is paying them must have run out of cash,' he said.

As they approached Neelgarh, they passed two outside broadcast vehicles parked in the lee of a crumbling wall. Local police constables had already moved them on earlier that day, but the vans had crawled back into the vicinity and now lingered in their new lair, the sunlight bouncing off their dishes.

'Bloodsuckers,' said Veerendra.

A girl carrying bottles of cola ran to the window of one of the vans.

'Enjoying the show,' he muttered.

The girl ran back to the provision shop.

'Bloody behenfuckers.'

Jyotsna had married Falguni's late father at the age of eighteen and had lived in a state of nervousness ever since. On her wedding day, she had vomited all over a ceremonial thali necessitating a separate pooja to quell the effects of the ill omen. She considered marriage a most unnatural state for a sentient being. What good could possibly come from being wrenched, at a sensitive age, from all that was familiar and then beached in a mansion full of strangers, tied to a bookish malcontent who would die at the age of thirty from an exhausted spleen?

Jyotsna's slender frame shrank over the years, her bracelets weighing down her fragile wrists like manacles. She developed a ghostly glide and began to whisper to dust clouds on the horizon. Her chest caved in on itself; her skin took on the pallor of decaying paper; her hair turned not white but a pale yellow.

When Falguni was first brought to Jyotsna, she looked into her little irises, quivering like drops of ink. The infant's heartbeat was enormous, her face a squalling reproof. Jyotsna held the child like an explosive – the child she had not asked for. She handed the bundle to the midwife and fell back onto the hot pillows, sinking under this new visitation.

Falguni was wearily claimed by her grandmother, assisted by a band of aunts. The mother was feckless. The girl was here. She had to be reared. They would do their best for her. That was the way of the Chauhans.

Jyotsna was left to her mysterious inner workings, her relationship with her daughter becoming ever more distant. A long period of silence between them would be broken by an oblique pronouncement from Jyotsna and, seconds later, Falguni's barbed retort.

When Falguni and Veerendra entered the haveli, Jyotsna appeared at the top of the staircase.

'I knew you would come to see me,' she said.

Falguni rolled her eyes.

The younger brothers' principal rooms lay on the first floor, facing the chequered flatlands to the west of the haveli. Jyotsna and Falguni sat in an alcove at the end of the corridor, a Dresden tea service on a low table at their feet. Behind them, a stained glass window mediated the sun's final rays, anointing Jyotsna's forehead with a crimson balm, preserving her lips in a ribbon of blue and laying a golden rhombus onto her tightly clasped hands.

'Are we going to talk about it now?' asked Falguni.

'I have not been avoiding it.'

'No one is telling me anything about it. Who they were, what happened to them. Nothing.'

'They are still trying to find out who they were. It takes time, I suppose. All those bones.'

Jyotsna reached out and turned the teacups so that their handles faced the same way.

'Who knows the truth?' asked Falguni.

Jyotsna's lips looked like they intended to form a word but her eyes were empty, bearing only a suggestion of an idea, too fleeting to lodge in her psyche.

'Someone here knows what happened. The press is saying that locals suspect that they are the bodies of Dalits who were killed on the orders of someone in our family. Thirty years ago something happened and it was all covered up, that's what they are saying. People don't just make up stories of this type. I mean, the evidence is there in the ground for all to see,' said Falguni.

Jyotsna shook her head sadly, a gesture as ambivalent as it was theatrical.

'How were they found?' asked Falguni.

A glow flickered back into Jyotsna's eyes.

'In the last year they have been fighting over that land, your uncle and the new MLA. Something about it being common land required for social development. We all know what that means. I could not believe it either, the gall of these good-for-nothing hoodlums. Times have certainly changed. I suppose they think that they have support in very high places. Well, someone from their side must have begun to build illegally, so they started digging. Late at night so no one would see. And by morning they had found them.'

Jyotsna took a deep breath. It had been a while since she had spoken for so long.

'And now look,' she said, 'we are here and they are there.'

She waved at the window, indicating the land outside.

Night had fallen. Beyond the stained glass window, high above the black earth that swept towards the sodden clay of the riverbank, pale points of light lay dusted across the sky.

Jyotsna reached out and eased her daughter's glasses off her face with both hands.

'Why don't you wear contact lenses?' she asked.

Falguni looked at her mother, her naked eyes large and unblinking.

Then she took her glasses back.

'There is something really wrong with all of you,' she said.

A moment later, slipping the glasses back on, she added: 'All of us.'

Breakfast was always served in a little recess called 'the sun room'. The light poured down through a skylight and was seized by the cutlery, the upholstery and the parquet. The others had all left the table but Veerendra was still there, chewing with the concentration of a dumb animal.

Falguni nearly turned back but he saw her and made a big show of swallowing.

'Nice of you to join us,' he said.

He called out for more bacon. Then he picked up a piece of toast, running his tongue over his teeth after each morsel, reaching into the far corners of his mouth.

'I need to see dadiji,' said Falguni.

'Your grandmother is not well enough to see you at the moment. She will get excited and that will not be good for her condition. Leave it a few days, let her get used to the idea.'

'What idea? Am I some sort of ordeal that she has to get used to?'

'Just give her a little bit of time.'

'You can't prevent me from seeing her.'

'Where is the question of preventing? We cannot afford to have her subjected to these obsessions of yours. I do not have to remind you that she is nearly ninety.'

'No, you do not have to remind me.'

Veerendra put his fork down and leaned forward.

'I am only going to ask you this once. With what right have you come here, asking questions, making assertions? Your head is not here, your heart is not here.'

'I am not having this discussion with you. All I want is to see dadiji.'

'Fine, don't have this discussion with me. Have it with the police, the Dalit Samiti, the press, or any other rotting motherfucker that you choose. But just remember this: once you get stuck with these matters, they will never leave you alone. You will spend your days waiting outside offices, you will be hounded night and day, you will weep with frustration. They will take your passport. They will make you run behind them like a stray dog. And all this will happen even if I don't lift a finger.'

He indicated the stretch of countryside through the window.

'Ask yourself where you are. Ask yourself who you are. This good life you enjoy and how you came to lead it: ask yourself about that too. And when you are satisfied, you can start all your interrogations.'

As she sipped her tea, Falguni kept her eyes lowered, choosing to take in only the filament of honey trailing across the tablecloth, the crane that was about to take off at the base of the teapot, the plate of heart-shaped apples that shone like metal. She added another spoonful of sugar to her cup, and then one more.

There were a few moments of relief when a maid came in to clear some of the plates. Her motions were quick and precise, her eyes downcast.

Falguni stole a look at Veerendra and he was still chewing. His thick eyebrows had begun to sprout their first grey hairs: the same woolly arches that she recognized in some of her male cousins and in photographs of her dead father. She pushed her chair back with a screech and left the room.

Falguni knew that before the morning prayers would be the best time. She walked down the corridor that led to her grandmother's room. Landscapes in gilt frames lined the wall at regular intervals, settings that could have been anywhere: sludgy swirls that passed for terrain, trees of little determination and clouds fading into the canvas.

There was only one light on the landing, and her grandmother's door lay in deep shadow. She pressed against it gently and listened. Then she knocked.

'Dadiji,' she called.

She jiggled the latch.

'It's me. Falguni.'

There was no response.

She played the child's game of walking away and then standing very still, her breath held. She wanted to count to twenty-one, the magic cipher, pausing for two blinks of an eye between each number. But instead, she went back downstairs.

The afternoons in the haveli were thick with a syrupy somnolence. Bamboo screens dropped over the balconies, throwing out clouds of dust, and the fans in the corridors were set to a low whirr. Aunts disappeared into their bedrooms, cousins napped on the sagging sofas in the verandas. The servants dragged the dogs to the kennels by the orchard and then confined themselves to the outside kitchen. Even the flies retreated into dark corners, blind with a post-prandial intoxication, too bloated to take flight.

Falguni lay on a swing outside her room, its curved sidebar cold and cruel as it cut into the back of her neck. Between each exhausted creak of the swing's hinges, the only sound she could hear was a faraway pounding: a mallet on grain, a sari on stone, a stave on flesh? She brushed the thought away and reached for her phone.

She looked for news on the grave, clicking away from site after site, impatient with the time they took to load. Then she paused.

On one of the sites there was an extract from a preliminary forensic report into the deaths:

> Bones corresponding to at least eleven individuals were found at the target site. The investigation was hampered by the extreme fragmentation of some of the bones, whether due to natural or unnatural causes yet to be ascertained. Assessment of craniometric variables in seven cases suggest male characteristics and in four cases female characteristics. Perimortem fractures are present in numerous bones and, where cranial, can probably be said to represent the cause of death.

She continued to look for media reports on the grave. This time, along with the search terms, she typed her own full name.

The driver stopped at Lala Kishanchand's provision store, an enterprise that seemed as old as trade itself. Sacks of onions and garlic were crammed under the wooden counter as they had always been, and the attached lean-to still housed pyramids of timber, metal rods and sandbags.

A sari, hung out to dry from an upstairs window, twisted in the wind.

Falguni was relieved to be in the centre of Neelgarh, pitched in its easy rhythm, away from the high walls of the haveli. She stretched out in the back seat and watched a family of sparrows bathing in a puddle under a handcart.

The driver returned and stuck his head through the open window.

'Someone from the shop wants to speak to you. Shall I send him, if you have no objection?'

Before she could reply, a figure emerged into the sunlight, head engulfed in a knitted hat, a shawl wrapped tightly around the torso, fragile ankles emerging from under the dhoti.

'Who is that?' asked Falguni.

The driver shrugged.

The man shuffled towards the car, chappals dragging, his body at an awkward tilt. As Falguni watched, the dhoti began to sag and slip, one end trailing in the dirt, threatening to gape wide open.

Falguni looked at him with panic. The man would be standing in front of her, half-naked, humiliated, bewildered, and somehow, she would be to blame.

Glancing down and deftly gathering the folds of his dhoti in one hand, he walked to her side and bowed his head.

Falguni opened the door and stepped outside.

'Pranaam,' he said, unconcerned by the state of his dress, 'you should not have got out. The sun is still high.'

Falguni was silent.

'I heard that you had come and I just wanted to rest my eyes on you for a second, so many years have gone by,' he said.

Falguni forced a smile: 'That is kind of you.'

'I have seen so many of you grow up in front of me. Even your father, God give peace to his soul. You know, your grandfather once had tea in the shop.'

'Really?'

'I promise, I would not lie. Here, look at this.'

The man held out his arm, his eyes discs of delight behind his thick glasses.

'Your hand?' Falguni asked.

'No, the watch, the watch.'

He rubbed its face against his shawl and presented it to Falguni again.

'It's a nice watch,' she said.

'Why would it not be? Do you know who gave it to me?'

'No.'

'Your grandfather. That time, after he had tea in the shop. And still, not one thing wrong with it. In all this time, I have only had to repair it once. That is the kind of man your grandfather was.'

Falguni nodded, still looking at the cracked leather strap, barely distinguishable from the man's skin, the plexus of veins bunched at his wrist, the lines that speared up towards his palm.

'Thank you for remembering him,' she said.

'That is what our teachings say, to remember those who have left us.'

A chill snaked down Falguni's back.

'God keep you safe,' he said, turning away from them, still holding up his dhoti.

Close to the Lala's store, there stood a circle of plastic chairs, a few half-empty glasses of tea planted in the soft earth beneath them.

'Can you ask someone what was happening here? That meeting?' Falguni asked the driver, pointing to the chairs.

'Must be something to do with the panchayat,' he said.

They returned to the car and made their way back along the village's only road, under a canopy of old campaign banners, still in place many months after the election. Thick curls of smoke from piles of burning leaves drifted past dark doorways. A group of men played cards under the thatched roof of a tea shop. Shopkeepers waved at the car, their faces framed by strings of shampoo sachets.

At the outskirts of the village, where the last houses clustered at the edge of the fields, part of the road had collapsed into a mound of rubble. A man on a motorbike blocked the narrow breach, his shoulders jerking as he worked at getting his engine started again. The driver let out a few sharp blasts of the horn just as the motorbike roared to life again. The man turned his head and seemed to look deep inside the car, past the driver, into the back seat, at Falguni. He threw his head back and spat forcefully into the scree at the side of the road before riding off into the farmland.

'These people have no respect,' said the driver. 'What can you expect?'

Falguni looked at the squat buildings on either side. There were gashes in walls where bricks had crumbled away and cracks in doors where the wood had warped. Windows stared and porches creaked. Shadows were cast down from the flat roofs under a sinking sky. She knew that there were eyes everywhere, peering at the car from each aperture, witnesses to the man hawking out his contempt, heads full of knowledge that slipped behind pillars and below sills, waiting for her to return to the bulwarks of her haveli.

The car moved forward and turned into the main road, Krishna and Radha bobbing their heads under the mirror.

Falguni, like many of the younger members of the family, had pieced together a sense of her grandmother's identity only through inherited memories and partial deductions. The old lady had been a vital presence of their youth, but occupied and elusive. They were aware that she had seen off her husband, four children and countless acquaintances. They knew that she had arrived at the haveli as a girl, curious and unformed. They realized that it was the family's good fortune that she turned out not only to be more shrewd and industrious than any of the Chauhan brothers, but that she also possessed the caution to disguise these qualities.

She did not require more than five hours of sleep. With the time gained, she was able to assert her position among the women of the family, regulate a galaxy of household matters and pore over deeds and accounts after her husband had gone to bed, a tightly rolled sari blocking out the trace of light under the library door.

She was a virtuoso in maintaining appearances. She picked her saris with prudence: cream, ivory and blush, colours of purity and capitulation. On full moon nights, she played the sitar on the terrace.

These days, she left the impression only of a presence that was fading away or a life that had never been. It appeared to the world that in her final days she had elected to retreat to her room, seeing in it some nook of childhood, a place of virgin experiences. She gazed with wonder at objects that had been in her possession for over fifty years: an ivory paperknife, a jewellery box inlaid with mother-of-pearl, gold opera glasses. She tickled herself with a fan of peacock feathers, her arms twitching with pleasure. She turned her head and the splendour of her rooms filled her with awe.

Veerendra now vigilantly controlled access to his mother. He went to her room every morning after the nurse had taken away the breakfast tray, spent twenty minutes or so behind the closed door and then returned downstairs.

'With God's help, she is pushing on,' he would announce.

When Falguni walked into her grandmother's room, the haveli was yet to stir. The nurse was asleep on a small bed in the antechamber. Falguni tiptoed past her and towards the chair facing the balcony doors. Her grandmother was already up and dressed, her head just emerging over the top of the chair's elaborately carved back.

'Who is there?' she asked, without turning her head.

'It's me. Falguni.'

Her grandmother waved her forward impatiently.

'So, finally, you have remembered me.'

Falguni crouched at the old lady's feet and smiled at her.

'How are you feeling? They told me that you might not be well enough to see anyone.'

'I can dance around this room like a girl of sixteen. Shall I show you?'

'No. Because I know you'll make me dance with you.'

'Come.' The old lady gave Falguni her arm. 'Let us move there.'

Her skin was cool and dry, as if it had been stored with care in a dark drawer, pressed between sheets of tissue.

Falguni settled her on to the sofa, tucking her shawl over her shoulders.

'Go and close that door. That girl is probably only pretending to be asleep.'

Falguni did as she was told.

'Good,' said the old lady when Falguni had sat down next to her.

She took her granddaughter's hand in both of hers.

'What a shock she will get when she comes in here,' she said, looking at Falguni with giddy delight.

'Good,' she said again.

Falguni looked down at the fragile hands that held hers, the fingers and nails that looked as though they were made of thin, tarnished glass.

'How old are you now?' her grandmother asked.

Falguni staved off the line of enquiry.

'Can I ask you, Dadiji, how long since you came to this haveli?'

'This is a real test. But I can tell you. Seventy-six years.'

'The British were still here then.'

'They were everywhere else, but they were not here.'

The old lady stamped on the carpet.

Falguni paused and then straightened her back.

'You have seen everything that has happened here since then,' she said. 'I don't know if anyone has told you about what they have discovered here. The grave.'

The old lady's features hardened, the folds of her face standing firm, the crevices filled with defiance.

'So this is why you have finally come to see me.'

'You know about it?'

'Yes, I know about it.'

Falguni pushed herself: 'You have known about it all this time?'

The old lady shuddered.

'You people will never understand about those days. The whole country was turning upside down. No one was working. The trains were not running. The rains had failed. Villages were on fire. No one knew what Indiraji would do next and what would happen here. Your grandfather was in Delhi, with not even a moment's peace, and I was here with your uncles. In the middle of all that turmoil, people tried to take advantage. We had become lax, I suppose. Before we knew it, these people turned up with some strange papers, saying that they now had the title to the land they had been working on.'

'The people they found?'

'We had to explain to them that no authority can just hand them property that belonged to someone else. That belonged to us.'

'This was all about the land?'

'When is anything not about land? What happened should not have happened, but they were playing with fire.'

'So how did they die?'

'We all die according to our destiny. We tried to help them but they pushed too far. If you start a battle, you have to be prepared for the consequences.'

'Dadiji . . .'

'Just because someone taught them to tuck their shirts in does not mean that they are everything and we are nothing.'

The old lady's voice faded and her eyes turned liquid.

'Why have you come here?' she asked.

'I'm sorry,' said Falguni.

'Send that girl here.'

Falguni stroked her grandmother's hand but said nothing.

'Wake her up. She is not paid to sleep.'

The old lady pulled her hand away, laid it in her lap and looked in the direction of the door.

'Tell her this room is cold.'

The site of the mass grave was eight kilometres from the haveli, in a place of stumps and soil, no different from the many acres all around. Falguni had not attempted to go near the area. She had told the driver to take her to a different part of the Chauhan estate, a wide field striped with furrows, near a path that led to the riverbank. There she had stood with her face lifted to the wind, the canvas flailing across the top of the jeep.

She had waited for something to happen: for what mattered, what ruled, to reveal itself in her instincts. There should have been fever, an ache in the belly, stinging in the eye. The place where the bones were discovered was no different to the scene that surrounded her. She could have been standing on that very site. But all she could feel was the wind rifling through her hair and the sun warming her face.

It seemed inconceivable that this land held such horror in its heart. But she knew that when she returned home at a late and silent hour, staring at her through a skull's dark sockets would be proof that family stories could leak and corrode, that the familiar could become the unmentionable, that a personal history could be defiled beyond comprehension.

In the distance, a woman made her way across a ridge at the edge of the field, a load of kindling balanced on her head. She stopped for a moment, perhaps catching sight of the jeep, and then continued, her contours wavering in the midday sun. But she was not a puff of smoke or a wandering mirage. She was a woman who had run out of wood and was forced into the fields in the face of a sun at its zenith. Falguni watched the woman until she finally fused into the earth, the sky and the air.

An hour later, she was still staring at the spot where the woman had vanished.

'Madam, it's getting late,' the driver finally said with an apologetic shrug.

'I am sure you don't want to talk about it, but I'll ask you anyway: what are they saying in the village?' she asked.

'What is there to say, madam? So many years have passed since then. I have heard that when it happened people here did not speak of anything else. All day and all night, people discussed their disappearance.'

He paused and Falguni nodded to encourage him.

'I remember my father saying that they were all from the same large family, growing a few scraps wherever they could. There were two brothers that he talked about. One was a mild man with a beautiful voice, known all through the village because he was sometimes allowed to sing at functions. The other brother was a hothead and they say that was how all the trouble began. There were probably a few sisters too, I don't really remember.'

'Do you know what happened to them?' she asked.

He turned to look across the field.

'My father never knew. None of us did. A veil fell over the whole matter and no one mentioned it again until now. But some used to say that they drowned when their ferry came apart halfway across the river. Others said that they ran away to Gujarat to escape their debts. I have even heard that a golden ladder came down for them and they simply climbed up into another world. People will recount anything and believe anything to live in peace. That is as much as I know.'

Falguni nodded at him again and got into the jeep.

As they picked up speed along the dusty track, she had no doubt that she would soon be on her way back to Ithaca. In a few days she would be teaching her seminars again and continuing with the research for her book. There would be a grant application to make. There would be papers to grade. And just visible below her collarbone would be the leather cord that would singe her skin through the day and night, its battered disc with the four-armed goddess leaving a permanently seeping welt.

HERO

You must be curious about our world. I can understand that. You have probably heard all kinds of things: that we suffer savage beatings for the slightest of reasons; that we are secretive and follow our guru like fanatics; that at night there is dark mischief among the boys. In your place, I would probably be curious too. But the truth is much more ordinary. We live here like any group of young men that has to follow a certain set of rules. We train, we pray, we spar, we dream. Is it really so different anywhere else?

There is a strict system for our daily life: the cooking, the sweeping, the washing. This morning, Vikaas and I had to prepare the pit where we fight. We took it in turns, turning over the soil, lifting it out of the earth's lap and then laying it back down. Vikaas steadied my arm as I dripped ghee over the mounds.

'Not that much. It's nearly four hundred rupees a kilo now,' he said.

'Oh,' I said.

'And you're supposed to say the mantra at the same time. Not later, when you feel like it.'

He continued to watch me so I put the pot down: he could do it himself. I picked up the incense burner and trailed the curls of scent over the furrows of the pit, cupping the smoke with my hand, burying it in the ground.

Vikaas opened his mouth, as if about to point out something else that I was doing wrong, but I turned my back to him.

Guruji likes things to be perfect but he does not bother to nitpick about the incense and the oil and the ghee. He is concerned with the important matters: our dedication to our practice, our faith in the life we have chosen and our humility before God. He is serious and demanding but then what kind of a guru would he be otherwise? For more than a decade he was the most celebrated wrestler in these parts, and his father and grandfather before him. But at our akhara you will not see photos of their glory days on the walls.

'We must revere those who came before us but we must not lean on them. You are the future. I want to see your photos on these walls,' Guruji says.

I had been at the akhara for nearly two years when Ranjeet arrived. Even in his checked shirt you could see the kind of fighter he was made to be, the power and muscle thrilling under his skin. It was hot that day. His lips were slightly parted and he blew softly into the air. It looked like it was that gentle sigh that brought him to life, turning a marble figure into a man.

He had a detachment about him that none of us had ever seen in a new student. He threw his bag down on the ground as if he never gave much thought to where he slept or where he woke up. Even when he touched Guruji's feet, he did it with a sense of equality.

None of us could stop looking at him. Guruji introduced him to us as the son of his sister, news that was unsettling because we wondered whether he would get special treatment in spite of Guruji's reputation for fairness. In the akhara, you have to know your place in relation to every other person there. A boy's native place, family position and jaat; his ability in the pit and the number of times he has won at a dangal; his generosity, his weakness, his tact; you have to find out all these things without asking and then work them into the hours of practice, prayer and chores.

A few of the boys stepped forward to tell Ranjeet their names, and he half smiled and nodded but his expression implied that their names were no concern of his. He shook hands with only two boys, appearing to pick at random. Dharam was one of them.

He glanced at Dharam's wrist and said: 'Nice watch.'

Those were the only words he spoke that afternoon. Dharam looked like he had swallowed the moon.

I was the other. Maybe he picked me because I was the smallest, the one who stood furthest away. When he held my hand, the shake turned into something unfamiliar. I was embarrassed so I just looked down, not knowing what else to do. He curled his fingers around mine and did not let go for a few seconds. We stood there without speaking, our hands like twin creatures inhabiting the same shell. Then he dropped his hand and strolled back to where Guruji was standing.

Without even looking around, I knew that all the boys were sizing him up: because he was related to Guruji, because he could be the akhara's next big success, but more than that even, because he looked like he carried with him the knowledge of his own danger and let it spark into the ground beneath his feet. You could tell that those limbs had too much strength locked in them, that they could inflict violence for no reason, a violence that would be beautiful and overwhelming.

My father writes to me every month. I don't have to read his letters to know what they say: they are always exactly the same. I go through the motions of unfolding the paper and running my eyes over the lines every time. He tells me that they are all fine; that with God's grace the work in the fields is proceeding and that they want for nothing; that I should respect my guruji and do as he says; that my brother asks how I am and that my mother remembers me as soon as she opens her eyes in the morning; that there is nothing but good news from my sister in her husband's home; that I should write soon to tell him of my progress at the akhara. They are letters that reveal nothing but if I hold them up to the light, I can see my father hunched over, his lips pinched in concentration, his hand setting the hurricane lantern first to one side, then the other, then back where it was, as he writes each sentence as if for the first time.

You asked about my family. My brother is eight years older and he always seemed to be from another time, a boy who had half caught up with the previous generation. I was closest to my sister: there is only a year between us. She lived through the books she read, in a world where actresses knocked on hotel-room doors to give bags of cash to blackmailers, where truck drivers rescued pretty girls from abandoned factories, where businessmen were tied to drainpipes for days. If my parents ever caught her with those novels, they would have fixed her properly. But she was careful, hiding them behind a photo of Shivji or under some dead leaves in a broken pot.

That was all she thought about. While we sat high above the railway track or returned home through the bamboo groves with the buffaloes, she would tell me what she would put in a story if she ever wrote one. It did not seem to enter her head that the months were passing, that changes would come to our lives. And of course it happened. She was married off to a government official in Azamgarh, a big man with no neck. Since then I can't tell you how many letters I have sent her. There has never been a reply.

How do I explain to you the effect Ranjeet had on us? We had never seen a young pahalwan like him. In no time, he mastered one of the hardest lessons of kushti: the art of stillness. He would stand in the centre of the pit as if he had sprung from the soil. Much more experienced boys would give themselves away by the flicker of an eyelid or a spasm under the skin, but Ranjeet's stance would be inscrutable, a soundless beat. Then, the second the whistle rang out, he would lunge for his ferocious grip.

The clinch, Guruji said; always the clinch. It would determine the fate of the fight: how a wrestler's balance could be broken and his confidence annihilated. Ranjeet would dominate from that first moment, anticipating a sweep or a throw, taking advantage of a chink in his opponent's hold, lifting him up with only as much strength as required, throwing him down with fleetness and grace, and then scissoring his own legs into position to ensure victory.

At first, I stayed away from Ranjeet during practice. What would be the benefit of the weakest in the group being pitted against the strongest? It was enough for me just to see the shape of his bouts.

He was the one who approached me.

'Here,' he said, 'let me show you.'

He picked up two good handfuls of earth and rubbed them into my shoulders and arms, firm circles of grit and loam. Wiping his hands on my chest, he spun me around. A grain of sand was caught in his eyebrow and glittered like a jewel. He led me to a corner of the akhara and adjusted my posture, pressing down on my calves, raising my chin.

'Bend your knees lower,' he said, 'you need to get more spring in your thighs.'

The grain of sand was still stuck fast, shining above his eye.

'When you grab, push up from here,' he said, his hand gliding over his hip bone.

I breathed in.

'Look directly into my eyes,' he said, pointing with his fingers.

Before I knew we had begun, before I could make myself ready, he had pounced, the slickness of his sweat against my face, he had twisted my torso through his arms, my feet were sailing off the ground, heat streaked through my stomach, the world blurred red. My back would have smashed on to the earth, but he pushed his arm out to break my fall. Then he let me drop, but gently, the way you let go of a floating lamp on the surface of the water.

He was smiling as he stretched his hand out to me.

'Now your turn.'

My days were lifted by the new thrill of moving into Ranjeet's vision. My technique began to improve and I could see that I had some fire within me. Even Guruji noticed the difference, his pleasure momentarily softening his gaze. When I pulled the beam across the pit, levelling the soil before the day's practice, each tug was effortless, a stroke that beat away the weight of my father's expectations, the shadows of past failures, the mysteries of the world outside, all the things that made me anxious. I began to feel that it was here that I belonged.

Ranjeet's reputation kept growing. At one dangal, he won thirty thousand rupees. His photo appeared in the papers again and again, his chest covered in garlands or his arm held up in victory, always by someone else. We heard that in Varanasi a politician offered him a good job at his party office. I did not envy him his success, all these things that a hero enjoys in his orbit. I was happy that he had been spared the knowledge of what it was like to watch someone like him.

None of it really mattered to me, that is the thing. The crack of pain down my back, the heat that ate up my belly, the calluses cut in two, the tremble of muscles late into the night, the forecasting of defeat: as long as I had laid my head in its rightful place, I could forget it all.

One day, when I was sweeping out the courtyard, I heard a sharp blast from the other side of the wall. A few seconds later, the whistle pierced through again. It could only have been Ranjeet.

He was waiting for me at the bend in the road, sitting astride a motorbike. When he saw me approach, he ground it into gear and it rattled and groaned like a dying man.

'Come on,' he said.

I hung back and could not stop grinning.

'Where did you get it?' I asked.

'Has that got anything to do with you?'

'But whose is it?'

'It's better if you don't know.'

'Did you steal it?'

'I'm not going to ask you again. Are you coming or not?'

I got on, my mind full of Guruji, the broom I had just stupidly left lying in the middle of the courtyard and a sweet sense that anything could happen.

'I don't think it will make it to the main road,' I said.

'If it does, you can press my feet for a month.'

The bike jerked forward and almost threw me off. We wound around the potholes, the engine still choking, refusing to give in quietly. I twisted around to see whether anyone had heard the noise and come out to investigate; but there was no one in sight.

'The only way is to trick this bastard,' Ranjeet said.

He slowed down until we had almost come to a halt and then suddenly accelerated. We shot over the ruts in the road, scattering clods and pebbles, the bike's roar locking us in its grip. We screeched and skidded and turned into a track that sloped down through the long grass, a steep plunge that pulled with all its might, through clouds of butterflies that parted like a yellow sea. I let go of his shoulders and crossed my arms across my chest. I stretched out my legs and arched my feet. I tilted my head back until all I could see was the hot, white sky.

I can't remember exactly when everything changed. I understood that people could get tired of one another, their interest could move on. Ranjeet and I spoke less and less. Many times I found myself at dusk swinging and straining in the gloom of the back wall, dragging myself up the rope above the platform, lying exhausted, knowing that he was no longer anywhere in the vicinity.

I have to tell you about what happened with the club. We use dumb-bells here but we also have the maces and clubs that you see pahalwans carrying in old photos. There is one club, as heavy as a young boy, a great monster with red rings painted around it. Even Dharam struggles to lift it to shoulder height, his face twisted like a beast.

One morning, Ranjeet put his foot on the club and called me over.

Then he said loudly: 'Go ahead. Show us. Lift it.'

I did not understand: 'What?'

'You were boasting that you could lift it above your head with one hand. So lift it.'

'When did I say that?'

'If you've changed your mind…'

I should have just walked away but a group had now gathered, I had already lost two bouts that morning and the thought came into my head that maybe I could, for just one second, heave it right up.

So I rubbed sand on my palm, gripped the handle and lifted. At first, the club rose easily enough but when it was level with my groin, my arm began to shudder and a hot charge began to run from my wrist to my neck. It seemed so important now, I kept going. Ranjeet's face had an expression I had never seen before: he was mesmerized by the sight of that club. I managed to bring it up to my stomach, then my chest, then my shoulder. After a couple of seconds, it slipped from my grasp and fell on the ground with a heavy thud.

Normally, there would have been hooting, joshing, jeers. But Ranjeet just looked at my shaking fingers, sucked in his cheeks and walked away. The others followed his lead, silently drifting off, to the back wall, to the platform, to the courtyard. I was the only one left in the centre of the room, spokes of light streaming in through the high windows all around, the club lying in the dirt at my feet.

When I looked up, Guruji was standing a few steps away. But it was not me that he was looking at. He was staring at Ranjeet with a look, the only way to describe it is a look of fear, a look that I thought I understood, and then did not understand at all.

There was more to come. A dead rat landed in my lap one night after we had eaten, flung by a figure that ducked too quickly for me to see. In my bed roll, I found a leaky plastic bag containing an inch of spit, collected over who knows how many days. A week or so later, Dharam handed me my blue shirt, soiled and torn, found under a bush outside the akhara. At least that was what he said. I had no proof that Ranjeet was behind any of these things; I am only telling you what happened.

I did not know how to ask him if I was being punished for a crime I might have committed. Everything was a question now. Nothing could make me understand his destruction of our bond.

Not every night, but often, I wake up uneasy, a tightness in my chest, knowing that during the day I have not prayed enough to Hanumanji. I pull myself up and sit with my back straight because it is not respectful to pray when you are lying down. I try to avoid disturbing Vikaas.

Then I begin to pray for my parents and my brother and their future; I pray that I hear from my sister and that her news is only good; I pray for Guruji's happiness; I pray not to be frail; I pray not to be selfish; I pray not to disappoint anyone; I pray for better powers of concentration; I pray not to spill my seed; I pray for help when there is too much quiet and contemplation; and when I cannot think of anything else, I ask to be forgiven for the thoughts that Hanumanji knows about but that I will not mention again, since recalling them may count as a double sin.

Then I slide down on to my back, the sheet tucked firmly under my heels, the night blacker than the world behind my eyelids. When the mosquitoes come I let them whine and bite and I don't scratch because the itching is something that I have to bear. I know that even if there is no one else, I can always talk to Hanumanji. But as I wait for unconsciousness, the silence troubles me even more than before. On some nights, it draws itself together, steps over the sleeping shapes in its path and prepares to lie down on top of me.

'Someone was here looking for you,' Ranjeet said one day after practice, squinting under his raised hand.

It had been more than three days since he had said a word to me or even looked in my direction.

'Who?' I asked.

'Your sister.'

'What?'

'Your sister.'

'That's impossible.'

He shrugged, turned away from the sun and let his hand drop. He cracked his knuckles and then tucked the tips of his fingers into his langot. A golden light struck his arm and the rounded bulge of his shoulder; tiny hairs glowed on the edge of his ear; a lick of sweat shone on his neck. He looked like he was going to walk away.

'Wait,' I called and held his elbow to stop him.

He jerked his arm away and turned to look at me, straight in the eyes.

'Did she tell you she was my sister?' I asked.

'How else would I know, fool?'

'What did she look like?'

'Young, I don't know. Look, I'm just telling you what she said. No need to question me.'

'Was she alone?'

'No, some man was with her. It looked like he was her husband. Big man.'

'Did she say anything else? Did she leave a note?'

'No, but she said they would be back later. At about seven.'

'How did she seem?'

'How the hell would I know? What do you carry around in that head of yours?'

He shook his head, his lip curling up, like nothing could help me, nothing would make any difference to the opinion he had formed of me.

'Seven tonight?'

He walked away without answering, his body dark against the sky, which was blazing with all the colours of evening. I watched him until he disappeared through the door of the akhara.

I made my way to the stone ledge around the peepal tree, and sat there with my chin resting on my knee, my hand massaging the sole of my foot, the flesh that creases up sometimes with a cold, sharp cramp. The air was beginning to lose its heat and I knew I should go inside and put a shirt on. But I stayed, weaving together possibilities that had brought my sister here and then unpicking them because each one seemed more appalling or absurd than the last.

At nine, I was still sitting on the stone ledge, hugging the hardness of my shins, stupefied by the wait, the cold, and all the stories trapped in the threads tied around the tree's trunk, each one a prayer, for a child, for a cure, for consolation.

I can see what you're thinking. What an idiot this boy is, to believe anything he is told, to humiliate himself like that. You are thinking: it takes a special kind of fool to be like this boy.

When I finally went back into our room, the light from the moon made the other boys look like strange animals washed up on a riverbank, things to be poked at with a stick. There were coiled legs, shining backs and dark, drooping heads. I crawled on to my bed roll, the stale warmth of the room loosening the blood in my temples. I knew it was late, very late, and that I would be tired in the morning, slow and distracted when it came to training. Lying on my stomach, I pressed my face against the sheet, feeling its rough weave against my lips. I did not want to turn over. I was sure I would see Ranjeet, sitting up in his corner, leaning against the wall, his face cut up by shadows.

I knew that something bad would happen that day. Guruji tells me that I need to develop my instincts and have a better grasp of the signs people betray. I know I am bad at seeing clues. Maybe you won't believe me but on that day I knew: there was a damp pressure in the air, a suffocating mass that matched the weight in my stomach.

I was collecting husks, twigs, small branches, anything I could get my hands on. I bundled them on to the rack of my bicycle and tied them tight with twine. Wherever I looked, the signs were there. The clouds seemed to be filled with dread and there was a new menace in the animal trails that led into the brush.

I was wheeling the bicycle back up towards the fields when I saw Ranjeet.

'Where are you going?' he asked.

I kept moving.

'To town, to the shops?'

I quickened my steps.

'To buy bangles?'

'To buy a bindi?'

'Some red to put on your lips?'

I could hear him running behind me, a lazy, goading pace that crunched the gravel.

'Maybe something to drape on those narrow hips.'

I let the bicycle go, spun round, lowered my head and ran at him, my shoulders wide, my arms braced. I heard the astonished whumpf from his throat as I crashed into his stomach and swept his legs into the air. A gull screeched and took off as we flew over the bank on one side of the path and landed in a narrow ditch.

In seconds, he had sprung to his feet but I was even quicker. I pushed the top of his head to one side making him lose balance, one or two more precious seconds gained.

The clinch, always the clinch.

I pinned his head under my arm and hooked his foot with mine. He stumbled. I slammed my weight down on to his side and he fell flat on his back, pulling me on top of him.

This was the day that I could read the signs.

He was wedged in the narrow base of the ditch. I pitched my body forward, pinning his arms with my knees and then leaned back so that his flailing would not throw me off. My limbs were all in harmony. I grabbed his throat, noticing, even in that ferocious instant, that the skin was like velvet. There was a dip at its base, perfectly formed to fit two thumbs that could press without pause.

He tried to jerk his head but it was not the movement of a human, maybe a fox or a bird. A thick tendon in the side of his neck bulged and bobbed; his eyes gave up their irises, holding only the whites; his legs thrashed in the watery mud. I should have heard gurgling or choking or spluttering from his open mouth. But the only sound in my head was a song, or part of a song, just a fragment, a high-pitched note held without variation, shrill, piercing, piping, long and loud enough to cancel everything else and convince me that I held the rounded edge of victory.

I don't know how long we stayed like that, me forcing, him yielding. Then, from a distance, I heard my name being called. And the sharp sound in my head stopped abruptly. I heard it again and again, my name, the wind fretting its edges.

I let go of Ranjeet and looked up. In the distance, on the bank, I could see Guruji running towards us. I had never seen him run before. He had the gait of a tall man: awkward, his long arms thrown up, his head jerking forward in heavy breaths. I saw that his running days were behind him.

Ranjeet was barely moving. His breath made a rasping sound, like bark being stripped from a trunk. There was mud in his mouth. The toes on one foot trembled.

I climbed out of the ditch and began to walk across the fields. I kept up a good pace and did not look back. All the way to the akhara, as I pushed through stalks and jumped over gullies, the knowledge that Guruji had finally seen me win a bout wormed itself into the front of my mind.

For weeks now I have had a fever that comes and goes, a taste of ash on the roof of my mouth and the same bad dreams. The doctor came and said it was nothing serious, that I should drink lots of water. He gave me some tablets that I crushed and rubbed into the wall.

Ranjeet is no longer here. There is so much speculation about what happened to him; day and night, there is not much else. Some people are saying that he was bitten by a snake and was transferred to a hospital in town. There are other theories: that he ran off with a girl, that he finally said something unforgivable to Guruji. No one here seems to think it is strange that I have nothing to say on the matter.

Guruji has spoken to me two or three times since I fell sick, but the conversation has always been about my health, my strength, whether he should ask my father to come and get me. I told him that my father would be disappointed if I returned home. Not forever, he said, only until you recover fully. Please let me stay here, I pleaded. He agreed but he had more to say. He will try and speak to me again.

Tonight I feel better than I have in a long time. You could say I feel well again. I noticed that the moon is almost full, with hardly a smear on its surface. The crickets are louder than they have been for a while. And the wind is still warm.

I think we need to start moving. Isn't that right? You said that the bus leaves at six. The walk there will take nearly an hour and then there may be a little bit of waiting. We have a long journey ahead. I can tell you the rest later.

THE POOL

Piggy Snout is wearing a leopard-skin one-piece today and I have to admit she looks good. Apart from the snout, but there's not a lot she can do about that unless she sees a surgeon. She is pointing at a daybed and getting one of the pool boys to adjust the canopy. He sets two yellow-and-white striped towels on the bed and puts a bottle of water into the basket by the planter.

I don't really understand why she has to come here. Papa is not around; can't she go to some other club? And if she has to be here, why does she have to come to the pool all the time, why can't she go and play tennis or fuck off to the spa? Actually, the club rules say that a guest can only be signed in when the member is on the premises. But when that member is Papa, I suppose it doesn't really matter what the hell the rules say.

She used to be married to Sanjay Sandhu, the scumbag that everyone calls Rocky, no idea why. God, as in Balboa? In his fucking dreams. Anyway, Sanjay-Rocky-whatever met a hot Harvard doctor in LA and that was the beginning of the end for Piggy Snout. Hee hee, can you imagine the look on her face when she found that out? Replaced by someone with an actual education.

Inder Pandey just dived in and now he's doing butterfly all the way down, taking up the whole pool, splashing like a whale. God, the things some people have to do to make themselves seem interesting. He went out with my cousin Sakshi last year but now they are giving each other some space. Meaning, he dumped her. It's more or less impossible to believe that they ever had sex. I swear to God, she's so OCD that she screams if you touch any of the photo frames in their house and, as for Inder, he's such a stupid oaf, would he even know where to put it?

I need to stop thinking about all these deadbeats and concentrate on my literature. I'd like to finish *The Color Purple* by the end of the week or at least by the time school starts. It's sort of confirming many of the things I know about men but I need to get to the end.

What a surprise, Shivani Anand is here today. Her dad is leaving her mum, the news about his chakkar with

Dolly Mehra has been everywhere. So gross, the sheer size of him, I don't even want to think about it. Dolly would definitely have to be the one on top. Shivani is making the biggest drama out of the situation. Honestly, this divorce is the most fabulous thing that has ever happened to her. You can tell that she thinks it makes her seem intriguing and complex. She has started wearing these crappy vintage glasses and a revolting puffy skirt. God, she really needs to stuff her attitude up her gaand, like she's so fucking unique, the number of kids with divorced parents just in this one stupid club.

I was a lot younger when Mama and Papa split up. It was a complete non-event, I'm not even sure I noticed. Okay, maybe it would have been cool to be in the middle of some kind of super-glam custody battle, but it totally didn't happen. To be fair to Mama, there aren't many people who would get into any kind of battle with Papa. But she could at least have given it a try.

Mama lives in London now and actually has a job. Everyone thought she would remarry but she has completely reinvented herself out there, works for a property company, drives a Mini, has hair like Halle Berry, which totally doesn't suit her by the way. Her flat is cute but it's tiny. I've only been there once because Papa doesn't like it – I'm supposed to see her whenever she visits Delhi. But who can blame her for not coming to this fucked-up city.

Mrs F is in charge of our house here. She was our housekeeper when Mama was around so I guess she was in charge then too. I used to call her Parvin Auntie but a couple of years ago I decided that I would start calling her Mrs Fardunji. It's so much more dignified. As far as I can tell, she spends most of her time getting Somu, our cook, to whip up all her favourite dishes. She doesn't think much of Piggy Snout and the feeling is mutual. I can tell.

Piggy Snout used to be a model and then a jewellery designer or interior decorator, the usual shit. Papa met her at a charity polo match; how fucking original. Didn't something like that happen in *Pretty Woman*? So Piggy's lucky day: she's not left his side since then. She has a son called Jay who's nearly three, or is it four? Who the hell knows. He really looks like her, although, luckily for him, not the nose. His hair is longish and wavy so he has a bit of a rock star thing going on. Apart from the little rings of fat around his ankles. I'm surprised his crazy anorexic mum isn't feeding him spinach soup all day. He's playing with one of the pool guys now, running a toy car all over his back, then trying to undo his laces.

Time to go. I don't want to get stuck in the evening traffic. Anyway, I'm so fucking sick of this place. I swear, I'm never coming back again.

Okay, total mistake coming back. All morning Piggy Snout's been trying to talk to me and now there's no peace even when I'm having my lunch.

She sits down opposite me and gestures to the waiter to tell him she has moved.

'Can I?'

She picks an olive off my plate and pops it into her mouth.

'Why don't we go shopping one of these days, you and me?' she asks.

'No thanks.'

'Come on, we can go wherever you want. Emporio maybe, or anywhere else you want.'

'Papa and I went to New York in December. I've got everything I need.'

The waiter turns up with her Caesar salad.

'Look, darling, it'll be fun. I know about these things. I'm sure you won't mind me saying, but I get the feeling that the bras you wear are the wrong size. It is so important to be fitted right, it changes everything, your shape, your posture, your whole look. I know it sounds ridiculous but trust me on this one.'

Her phone beeps and she checks her messages. The ends of her hair are just touching the puddle of dressing on her plate as she leans forwards and smiles at her screen.

I give up on lunch and go to the changing rooms. There is a vase of camellias by the folded hand towels, and framed pencil sketches of women with cigarette holders on the walls. The place smells of moisturiser and chlorine. I check out the silver clasps on my bikini bottoms in the mirror. The passage behind me leads to the whirlpool, a place where hardly anyone goes because it's so dark and airless. I feel like I am waiting for something to happen. I open the door to the steam room, but it's empty.

When I come back out, the sunlight is blinding. The pool looks like a sheet of white metal. I have to walk past the tables where the boys hang out, their bodies so ridiculous, all toothpick legs and flipper feet. They are basically just a bunch of perverted pigs who are too slimy to have girlfriends and too dumb to have discovered drugs yet. God, they talk enough shit as it is, can you imagine them on coke? As my cousin Sakshi might say, fucktard central.

Over in the big cabana is where the Aunties congregate. They would be so horrified to be called that. It's shaded from the sun so they won't get dark and it's near enough to the champagne bar. They are all newly-weds, diamonds the size of grapes, so much make-up they can hardly blink, so much Botox they can hardly crap. I suppose they have a window of two to three years to enjoy their security and status: in that time, they have to have children or they will be shown the door. Some poor bitches will have the children and still be shown the door. Hee hee.

Jay has spread all kinds of plastic junk on my lounger. I flick it all on to the ground but he just picks it all up and puts it back there again. He's so annoying. And his face is really too much like Piggy Snout's, it's freaking me out. I tip up the lounger, pour his shit on to the lawn and drag it to a spot two feet away. A pool guy comes running up to help but I just wave him away. I lie down on my stomach, turn my head away from Jay and hope he leaves me alone.

Last night, Papa and I had a huge fight. Okay, it was late when I came home but, honestly, who needs a panga at two in the morning? It wasn't even about where I was or who brought me home or anything like that. It was about values and appreciation and duty. I mean, all of a sudden, it was like Mother Teresa in a Valentino suit. He wants to tell me about duty? I just laughed in his face and decided to go to bed. But he wouldn't let me, he just went on with his lecture and all the time Piggy Snout was in the background, pretending not to be there, but loving every minute with that diplomatic, concerned, full-of-shit look on her face.

I called him a hypocrite, a liar and a fake.

He looked like he was going to slap me.

Then she looked so eager to participate, I thought why not, come and join in, have some fucking fun, and called her Piggy Snout to her face. In the heat of the moment, of course.

By this time, Mrs F was up, whining about something, still wearing that vile housecoat, Papa had grabbed my face and shouted at me to apologize and Piggy Snout was pretending to cry. Then Papa told me I could forget about Hong Kong. So the end result is that I have had very little sleep and am fucking exhausted this morning.

'Hi, Nams.'

It's that bhenchod Sahil Wadhwa. Even if all he says is hello, he can make it sound like full-on sexual harassment. I used to date his brother last year. Sahil is looking at me over his stupid shades like he knows everything about me, like it's all infinitely fucking amusing. I want to grab his head and smash his face down on the pretty mosaic tiles.

'So what's going on, Nams?'

'Don't call me Nams.'

'Arre, what's your problem?'

'I'm trying to read. You know, a book.'

'You're such an in-tull-ek-shual, Nams.'

'Could you please only talk to me when you're decent?'

'What?'

'Isn't that an erection?'

'Fuck you, slut. You've probably seen enough of them.'

'None that small, actually.'

At precisely what stage during adolescence do boys turn into complete assholes? Alice Walker is great and all, but she has not been of much help on this point.

Dimple Seth is at the outdoor shower, checking out her own body, feeling up her thighs, like she's auditioning for a porno. At her age. Her family's story is that she has been away in Arizona for some business meetings. But m'Lord, there are a few problems with that testimony. Point 1: Instagramming your boobs all day is not a business. Actually, scrap that, it totally is. Point 2: who the hell does business in Arizona anyway? And point 3: everyone knows it was rehab. She got back about a month ago and Adi was saying she has found herself some baba down south to be her new spiritual adviser. These people are all so fucking predictable they make me want to kill myself.

Back to *The Color Purple*. Shug has given Celie a mirror and tells her to look at herself down there. She is teaching Celie how to touch herself, how to enjoy it, how to expect more. They are all over each other, groping and kissing.

I'm wondering now, did Whoopi Goldberg actually do all this stuff in the movie?

Today did not start well. I felt so queasy in the morning and after breakfast I was sick literally all over the bathroom floor. Then I realized that I'd lost my phone, probably last night, and had to deal with that whole nightmare. Then Arjun called to cancel tomorrow night because his mum is making him go to a gallery opening and will freak if he says no. Don't worry, as soon as he manages to locate his balls I'll be the first to let you know.

Finally, just to top it all, Piggy Snout appeared at the club, dressed for a meeting or something, all smart trousers and super-high heels.

She walked right up to the cabana where I was squeezing the water out of my hair.

'I've come to talk to you, away from your father. It's time you learnt some manners and how to show people respect, you bloody brat,' she said.

We were both wearing shades: I couldn't see her eyes and she couldn't see mine.

'I have done my best to be nice to you but obviously that's not enough.'

The sprinklers were going crazy behind her, making big loops in the air.

'Your papa is under a lot of pressure right now, and it's in your best interests that you stop behaving like an infant.'

Her toenails are a sort of dark purple today. I saw the bottle in Papa's bathroom: Midnight Mulberry.

'Do we understand each other?'

I nodded slowly.

And then she left, tucking her bag under her arm, click-clacking all the way back to the clubhouse.

The Malkhani twins are here today with their fake accents and fake hair. They have been turning up to school with their bodyguard, a fatso who looks like he escaped from a Tamil movie. No idea what he does while they are in class. Can you imagine anyone wanting to kidnap those two, the way they never shut up about how they are all so close to the royal family in Monaco. Didn't that prince have a baby with some totally random air hostess? Classy.

Every conversation they have is basically the same. They could be talking about nail polish, traffic jams, cancer – doesn't matter at all what the hell it is. With their mouths open wide so you can see that gross wad of pink gum.

'I can't even.'

'Hashtag mindfuck.'

'Did you? Did I? Did any of us?'

'This. This. This.'

Every fucking time.

Lola Shariff is doing yoga on the grass. What she's actually doing is flirting with Sahil Wadhwa, flicking her hair, stroking her legs, arching her back, then she'll just get into a totally arbitrary yoga pose. Lookatmyasshole-asana. He looks like he's going to have a heart attack.

'Oh Jay, baby, what is this?'

Piggy Snout takes off her shades. Jay's arms and legs are

covered in strawberry milkshake, his hair matted with the stuff.

She starts to get up.

'Don't worry, Paloma, I'll take him,' I say.

She looks amazed.

'Are you sure?' she asks.

'It won't take long. I need to go anyway.'

'Thanks so much, darling. His bag is just there.'

She wags her finger at Jay and then smiles at me. Jay is happy enough to come with me, his hand all sticky and warm. The milkshake is dribbling down the side of his neck into his T-shirt and this seems to be giving him, like, the most ridiculous joy. He keeps trying to lick his own neck.

I look back to see if Piggy Snout is watching us. She is sitting on the daybed, talking to Mandira Thapar, nodding and smiling, her legs stretched out on the grass. Today she is wearing a silvery kaftan, Dior shades and a straw hat with a big brim. From here, with the sun behind her, she looks like a picture on a hoarding. All she needs is a tropical cocktail in her hand and a man in a white suit looking into her eyes. Welcome to Shangri-fucking-la.

I can't believe it. No sign of Piggy today.

Except that there's still no peace because Namrata fucking Das insists on lying next to me. She has somehow got herself involved with the foreign embassy crowd these days, so it's always the French ambassador this or the Canadian High Commissioner that. I mean, no wonder the world is in the state it's in. She's having a party at her farmhouse for a diplomat from Slovenia. Can she even point to it on a map? I wonder what they make of her. It's so embarrassing. They probably all go back to their countries convinced that India is full of brain-dead females who think Mussolini is a sauce.

One thing she has going for her is her husband; he really is pretty hot and looks about ten years younger than her. He was in the air force and I think he may have also done some modelling. I wonder what sort of adverts: maybe instant noodles. Or mouthwash. He has that squinty, minty-fresh look about him. When they do it, I'm sure she just sits back in her chair and he goes at her on all fours like an eager puppy.

That didn't last long; Piggy's back today. The sun is burning up my shoulders and neck. Jay's sitting in a tube and shrieking with delight as I push him around the children's pool. I keep going faster and he keeps yelling louder. We crash into inflatable dolphins, seahorses and turtles. I am holding the tube with both hands now and whirling him around on the water. He's still screaming as the world spins round and round in blue and green and yellow.

As we climb out, Piggy Snout starts to yell at Jay again. Okay, not exactly yell, more that firm-but-not-totally-losing-it growl she does so well because it shows good modern parenting. She actually sounds very creepy. I think I'd prefer someone to just start screaming and freaking the fuck out. At least you know where you stand. Anyway, Jay pissed her off big time by putting her handbag in the paddling pool. Who knows what was in there, since all her shit is at our place anyway. I guess there was the bag itself which, yup, essentially was some new season snakeskin shitbox. So, after she pulled him to one side and lectured him to death, he turned around to me and I swear he rolled his eyes. There may be some hope for the child after all.

'Jay-Jay,' I call.

He stumbles over, thrilled to get away from Piggy. I am going to help him improve his range of facial expressions. If you really want people to know what total fuckheads they are, it is best not to use any words at all.

'Do this,' I say to him, raising my right eyebrow.

He jerks his whole head upwards.

'Okay, let's make it simple,' I say, raising both eyebrows.

Once more, he raises his head.

'Just your eyebrows, doofus, not your head. Like this.'

The same again.

I touch his eyebrows with my thumbs and say: 'These things. Just use the muscles above them, man.'

He reaches up to my face, pinches my eyebrows and says: 'Here.'

This sad fucking kid. Not only Piggy's looks but her brains too.

I go for a walk around the pool. The pool guys wear shirts with pockets that are trimmed in the same yellow and white as the towels: I've never noticed that before.

Can you believe it's someone's job to come up with these things?

The stone path is insanely hot so I walk on the lawn, the grass still soft and wet from the sprinklers. At the edge of the pool, I take off my shades and look down into the water. It's sort of greenish today. Are these morons even cleaning it properly? I read a story about these bacteria that got into a woman's ear from the pool water. They swam down her ear canal and just stayed there eating and rotting the flesh until she went deaf or something. Even too much chlorine can be really serious. It burns through your skin and gives you breathing problems, making you choke or pass out. Then there was that boy who was crushed to death by the pool pumping system in a water park. Maybe the gate was loose or unlocked, he just got sucked into the place with all those wheels and pipes and no one knew where he was for ages.

I read today that Piggy Snout is opening a shop. A 'flagship store' she is calling it. She has roped in some Bollywood zero for the launch and probably ninety per cent of the people around this pool will make an appearance to congratulate her. At least for Papa's sake they will. She must have assistants and managers and staff because who is doing all the work while she's posing on her daybed?

I don't actually know what this shop is supposed to be selling. The profile piece in yesterday's city section said that the project will showcase an eclectic range of innovative accent pieces. Piggy Snout is known for her unique design sensibility and her refreshing approach to interior aesthetics, combining the contemporary and the traditional with vision and flair. There was a picture of her sitting in an old library. A library.

Anyway, so I finished *The Color Purple* today. It was great as it went along but the ending was pretty damn unconvincing. I didn't really see how Celie could arrive at that place of forgiveness after everything that happened to her. I mean, yes, I get it, she changed and had that awakening and took control of her life, but sitting there on the porch, reminiscing with that Albert about days gone by? No fucking way.

All day I've been sitting in the dark, the curtains drawn, the door locked. I told Mrs F and the maids not to disturb me under any circumstances and that they should leave my food on a tray outside the door. Room service. My eyes feel like they are going to fall out of my head, I've watched so many movies. All the downloads have sort of rolled into one so the mob boss is romancing the cheerleader whose mum got cancer after she came back from the hiking trip in the Amazonian jungle where the strippers shot the vampires.

I go out on the balcony for a bit of air and hear that siren still going. Someone is being robbed or attacked in this city and someone else is raising the alarm, as if a hero will really come to the rescue, as if anyone actually gives a shit. The watchman salaams me from the drive and I nod back. This one's been here a while but I bet he doesn't know my name – why should he? I don't know his. I have the worst headache and my jaw hurts from doing that teeth-grinding-chewing thing all night.

I just realized I have no idea what time or even what day it is. I'd check but I've lost my phone again. I know. For now, I would just be happy if that siren stopped screaming. I go back inside and lock the balcony doors and everything is quiet again, just the AC beeping every now and then. What's its problem? I kneel on the bed and wrap the quilt around me. Every time I close my eyes, I can hear splashing, see water rising, feel it filling my lungs. That's why I don't sleep.

The pool is still closed and no news on when it will reopen. But it's been raining for a few days anyway, nothing dramatic or exciting, just little drips and drops all day, enough to drive you fucking insane. School starts again next week and I've really got that sick feeling, a dread that anything can happen. Mrs F is being a total bitch as usual, and I am trying to stay out of her way. I think she had some of her awful friends here yesterday afternoon. She got Somu to make a fish thing and it stank out the whole house. This is the kind of shit that goes on when Papa is not here.

And all the media-wallahs have gone crazy. Apparently, there were reporters and photographers trying to get into the club and I know there were people here at the gates. I haven't left the house for a week.

Piggy Snout has had some kind of breakdown and Papa's taken her to a clinic in Switzerland to help her recover. They went about a week ago but it feels like longer. I have read about these places: they make you exercise in the freezing cold and do group therapy, draw pictures of your pain and act out your feelings, stuff like that. I wonder what the view is like from her window. Snow-covered mountains, the sun on the lakes, miles of green forest, I guess. Will she even be able to see any of those things?

A cleaner found Jay's body floating in the whirlpool in the women's changing room. He was still wearing his floppy red hat and sandals when they brought him out and laid him on the lounger. One of the pool guys had to take the hat off before trying to give him first aid. They rushed him to the hospital but there was no hope.

And everything's just been crazy ever since. But not really crazy, just insanely quiet, as if we're not in the real world any more. How does a kid even drown in one foot of water? I mean, if he fell in, wouldn't he have just climbed out? He was always jumping around and picking himself up everywhere else.

Because this is the thing, fuck, I swear it on my life, I really swear. I just wanted to scare him, tease him, trick him, I don't know, hear him wail because he was getting on my nerves. He was supposed to go and look in the whirlpool room and see that there was no fun surprise in there, nothing but dimness and that rushing water, then come straight out and hit me on the ass, like when he knows I've fooled him. That's all, I swear. But I just forgot. I played that game and then I forgot.

Papa said Piggy Snout will get better. She has to, he said, no matter how long it takes. I guess after that they'll get married and she'll come and live here. That was always the big plan; it had to happen. There's no way she will be the same person after all this. Maybe she'll try and open her shop again, I'll be back at school and Papa will be doing what he always does. I click on another movie and turn the volume up, leaning closer towards the screen, pausing and playing, biting the softness inside my lip until the skin breaks.

THE PHILANDERER

He had been married. Her name was Winnie and she had left him to join an old boyfriend in South Africa. Once he had recovered from the humiliation, he enjoyed telling the story. In some senses, he conceded to himself, she had acted wisely: his infidelity had begun some months into the marriage, and what they had mistaken for love had turned out to be a rather cold admiration for each other's intellect.

The divorce had been like an efficient demerger. They had retained separate legal titles to their properties and investments; they shared no bank accounts. They had a frank discussion about the art, after which she sold the Raza and he kept the Souza. She left him her late father's railroad memorabilia, only because she did not have the time to arrange shipping. He had no idea what she did with her cars but was glad of the extra space in the driveway. The subject of the loyalty of mutual friends had never arisen: he suspected that she had never cared for his; he had certainly not warmed to hers. They had never featured in each other's wills.

And so life proceeded, slipping past the markers to which he was accustomed: hearing dates, notices, adjournments.

He was an outstanding advocate, by profession and by predisposition, and as a result, was impossible to corner.

'Those were not my words,' he would say, 'they were yours.'

'You assumed that I would agree.'

'At no point did I state that.'

When he spun round in his office chair, through the large back window, he could see the sunlight steal along a row of sandstone arches, with their delicate pigeon spatterings. Air-conditioning units studded the brickwork and a sign for a rival law firm glowered over a pair of ancient windows. Further up, pots of red hibiscus stood behind the iron scrolls of a top-floor balcony. The rumble of traffic never reached him but he knew it was there.

When he spun back, he faced bookcases and armchairs in appropriately magisterial hues, the walnut and the burgundy that gave him such a sense of calm, the touches of gilt that lifted it into a gentle optimism. On the wall, there was a large map of the world. He felt that it was in the right place.

One of his most celebrated cases turned on his construction of the word 'it'. The judgement stated that the court was persuaded by his argument that the reading of the pronoun did not require a circumambulation that avoided the obvious. 'It' in this case meant what it was naturally intended to mean: in plain terms, 'it'. His pleasure on reading the decision was so keen that his temples ached in a way that was almost carnal.

When he looked at women, any appraisal he made was stately and urbane. There might be an extra blink, a minuscule lifting of the chin. At most, he would redirect his sight over his reading glasses, a shift barely perceptible to anyone else.

In that second, he would have seen it all: the intricate brown tints in a girl's eye; the soft dip where the neck curved dangerously towards the shoulder; the raggedy line of a bitten nail; the heavy bracelet that made a thin wrist look even thinner; the tapering of an eyebrow; the skirt wrenched over the hips; the lips that would pucker at the end of every sentence.

He knew not to be unkind – he would never comment on sensitive matters like weight, attire or the size of someone's nose. He furnished compliments, within reason. And he would not respond to bile. Did he enjoy the sex, pray tell? Would he like to return some day? But of course, only at his lordship's convenience. Was there anything else she could do for him, tie his fucking shoelaces perhaps?

It was kinder to just let the moment pass.

When the dense text on his desk overpowered him a little, he would lean back in his chair and cast about in his cache of memories. The ticklish nutritionist who would hiss angrily at her dachshund when it tried to join them in bed. The PhD student in Jadavpur who would devise leaden puns. And that sweaty woman who owned a harp.

An oncologist had flirted with him at a hospital in Alipore. Rounded and dimpled, she was a curious blend of daring and bashfulness. During sex, she would push him down on the bed and sit astride him, all the while hooting like an owl; but later struggle into her bra and panties for the five-foot dash to the bathroom.

At a literary festival, he had met an influential magazine editor with close-cropped hair and a beautifully shaped head. She wore a bespoke scent. That night he caught traces of it in the crook of her elbow and the dip under her collarbone – a hint of lavender and singed oranges. He was surprised that, in spite of being involved in publishing, she spoke entirely in clichés. Eventually, it became unbearable. And then she began to call him 'Bun', short for a mystifying moniker, 'Bunny'. They parted after an evening of bathetic passion on the vintage Chesterfield in his study, their skin clinging to the leather. He still thought about the shape of her head with a spasm of regret.

He dissuaded his partners from chatter during sex, whether it was talk of private parts, imminent manoeuvres or, more simply, praise. He found it gauche and distracting. But not everyone would comply.

'What this country needs,' one woman had said, her face glistening as she held on to the headboard, 'is more Muslims. Like you. Secular.'

Unwilling to respond at that precise moment, he said: 'I'm very close. Here, bite on my thumb.'

He had fifteen blue silk ties, each a slightly different shade of cerulean.

He was as discreet as he needed to be. His trysts were not too frequent and no one was permitted to spend the night. This was as much for his own felicity as his neighbours' satisfaction.

Like the limbs of a statutory provision, the elements of an affair needed separation, scrutiny and then synthesis. It was a question of logic, an assessment of risk. He had a fine instinct for action or delay, knowing exactly when the call needed to be made, the bouquet sent, the date arranged or, with a deadly precision, cancelled. He heard the viscous plea days before it was made, and by the time the angry accusation was hurled, he was unreachable.

There were women who would try and infiltrate his life, to slip by with a feathery casualness saying they had friends who lived on his road or wanted to consult one of his colleagues on a legal matter. The married ones would try to arrange dates for him with profoundly unattractive women, all the better to make themselves seem more desirable. They would hum and whirr for his benefit.

It was difficult for him to predict when he would tire of a lover, but when the moment came, he was flooded with relief. He had the sense that when the waters receded, all would be washed clean. And then he could begin afresh.

On occasion the parting was amicable, much of the time it was not.

'You disgusting bastard,' said one message on his voicemail, 'you wait and see, I will cook your bloody goose.'

He was fortunate that no one had ever made a scene in public. One night at the Tolly, a woman had spotted him in the Shamiana and made her way to his table. She stood just inches away, her face hardening like lime.

'Hello, Ruby, good to see you,' he had said. 'Do you know Rana and Mitali?'

She had given them a stony smile and then walked away, jostling against the table as she did so. Red wine sloshed on to his cuff. Later that night, he put the shirt in the bin.

He was a contented man.

She was not one of those women. Even when he asked for her number, she appeared curiously distracted. After their first encounter, he had suggested meeting again, accustomed to acquiescence, its eagerness sometimes manifest, sometimes cloaked.

She said: 'Why not? But let's see.'

She smiled but her expression was freckled with doubt.

And that demeanour persisted. As if she was aware that she was only a temporary feature in his life, but unconcerned because for her, too, the real prize lay elsewhere.

Over the years, he had needed to make enough careful adjustments to his own conduct and had learnt to be wary of preconceptions. He considered himself to be worldly. And yet her attitude surprised him. She had proved to be even more guarded than him, having made it clear at the outset that she would not answer personal questions or talk about her life. They both knew why they were seeing each other; better to leave it at that.

Out of the dozen times they had met, they had only ever arranged to see each other once in a public place. This struck him as odd – people generally wanted to be seen out with him. One evening he had insisted that they have a drink at a café before going on to his place. She refused and hung up, then called him a little later to say that she would come, but for no more than half an hour.

A few people glanced at him as they entered the café; with his height, that was not unusual. No one seemed to look at her. They sat at a table near the door. The light from the clusters of low-hanging lampshades softened her face but she still seemed ill at ease. She gulped her tea and her eyes flitted to the clock above the kitchen door, treating the place like a train station or a doctor's waiting room. They talked about the constant fog in the city and a fire that had broken out at a nearby building, whether they knew anyone affected by it. It seemed to him that they could just as well have been a couple exchanging dreary endearments on Valentine's Day or bickering about their dog.

Then he noticed a man a few tables away, sitting alone: his gaze would rest on her for a few seconds, shift and then return. There was curiosity in that look; no recognition but a sensual interest. The man had seen in her the same thing that he had noticed on that very first encounter. He felt a swift jolt of desire at this knowledge, an unrequired but potent confirmation. He made a signing motion to the waitress.

As they emerged from the café, they saw a man in checked trousers holding a giant inflatable fish. The fish wore heavy rimmed glasses. As they walked past him, they saw that he had a startlingly similar face: the same pursed lips, bulging eyes set wide apart, a gill-like crest of hair. He too wore heavy rimmed glasses. They were assailed by a puerile hilarity and hiccoughed all the way to his car. It was the only moment of levity in their relationship.

He never undressed her; he did not dare. Her movements were quick and economical, and she always put her sandals together in a corner by the wall. She was small and angular and reminded him of an implement that could be folded up after use. If one could find all the hinges.

Her only softness was the great billow of her hair. She wore it in a bun that she would undo with supreme efficiency, putting the pins into the side pouch of her handbag. Her hair would spill in dark gushes over her shoulders. When he lay on top of her, many wordless minutes later, her head having inched towards the edge of the bed, long strands would fall inkily towards the floor.

She had a staunch appetite and a bold reach. She showed no timidity about her body. Nothing would slow her down or make her pause, not the afternoon heat, not a pesky hair caught in her mouth, not the limitations of her own small heart. He would ignore his own urge as he watched her face play out the attainment of something elemental and vital, something possibly ruinous.

She always set an alarm on her phone before they had sex, a fact that greatly amused him. He wished he had thought of it first.

They had now been meeting for almost a year. He was on the point of mentioning this fact to her, but then decided against it. There was always a slim chance that even a woman like her could see that as some sort of amorous declaration.

He watched her as he knotted his tie. She straightened the bed covers, reaching over to the far side to smooth out a tiny crease under the pillow; she aligned a hardback with the fountain pen stand on the desk; she wound his belt into a tight roll and put it on the bedside table.

Then she caught his half smile in the mirror.

'What's so funny?' she asked.

'Nothing. It's just that you look like you're in training to be a chambermaid.'

She picked up her handbag and walked to the door.

Without turning around, she said: 'Don't call me again.'

He did.

Her taxi arrived at the gates a few minutes early.

He was tentative at first, wondering if she would still be taut and peevish, trying to glean something of her mood from the way she walked into the room and glanced around her. When she took off her blouse, he thought he saw a quiver beneath her breasts. Or perhaps it was his imagination, conjuring up a sign of a reticence that did not exist.

Later, as she slept, her lips parted and a frown flickered across her face. Her hand moved, forming a loose fist. It carried a latent energy, a force she was saving for another time, a time when she was not with him.

She was no longer a thing he could fold up.

Her fist unfurled.

And then the alarm went off.

He had never done anything like this before. When she was in the bathroom, he found a bank passbook in her handbag and copied down the address. The last entry was three months ago so there was a good chance that she still lived there. He had no intention of knocking on the door and throwing her life into disarray. He only wanted to see where she lived.

It was exactly what he had expected – a low block of flats in a quiet side street. He parked his car in a nearby road and walked the last few hundred yards. At the corner, there was a man on a stepladder stringing up lights over the door of a community hall. Girls in school uniform rode past in pairs, lunch baskets swinging from their bicycle handlebars. A cane sofa was having its seats restored on the pavement opposite the building.

A squawk drew his eye upwards. Washing lined most of the balconies but on one there hung a cage, its bad-tempered occupant craning its neck in his direction. He did not think she was the kind of person who would own a parrot. There was no one about so he walked towards the stairway and scanned the names on the mailboxes. He saw no indication of her. He walked backwards, still looking up at the building, and stepped into the shade of a rain tree.

Some minutes later, she emerged from the stairway, holding a knotted bag of rubbish. He could not look away, where would he look? She appeared exhausted, dark circles under her eyes, a facc thal seemed to have almost caved in on itself. She dropped the bag into a bin and turned to go back upstairs.

There was no rational choice, only the coarsest impulse. He followed her.

At the landing she must have sensed his presence. She spun round and he thought she would scream. But instead, she trembled with rage.

'How dare you,' she spat, 'how dare you come here.'

Then there was a crash that came from the flat on the other side of the landing, its door ajar.

'Ma?' she said, rushing back in.

As he entered the flat, the odour hit him first: an unpleasant vaguely medicinal smell, made worse by airlessness. The room was dark. He tried to isolate the smell's constituent elements – antiseptic, menthol, old grease. And beyond that, the smell of chai that had been left on the hob too long, that had boiled and boiled and risen and spilled and burned to a muddy crust.

The room was long, punctuated by sideboards and cabinets, dusty plants, nests of tables. Everything had at one time been correct; but since then had buckled. At the far end there was a smear of brightness, through the balcony doors.

There was a sound from a corner of the room, a little bit of a whimper.

He had expected children, perhaps a whole raucous litter, a glum husband or even another lover, but not this.

A couple sat at a table in the gloom. Even at this distance he could tell that they were ancient and broken. Their heads were hard and spare against the light from the balcony, more bone than skin. Their shoulders were fragile, their necks bowed. A glass from the table had fallen to the floor.

'Never mind,' she said, squatting with a dustpan and brush, 'it's only a glass.'

Her mother looked at her and the brush with no recognition or comprehension. The old man ignored the scene completely, his head bobbing as he seemed to fall back into sleep.

'It's done now but don't stand up. I'll just make sure there's nothing in the corners,' she said.

They had not heard or maybe had not understood her. In any case, they did not give the impression of being able to stand unassisted. The old woman put her hands on the table, the skin thin and cracked, the fingers with the yellowing sheen of age. She looked at him as if he were a scene framed for a moment in a window, nondescript and fleeting. Then she looked at the place where the glass had been.

'Let me just sweep up this last bit, then I'll get you that banana.'

The front of the old man's shirt was mottled with drool, his chin falling into sad folds of flesh.

'Here you go, you like soft fruit, don't you?'

It was all so different from her usual crisp, urgent remarks. Her voice was deeper and softer, her gaze moving from one part of the room to another, as if this were a monologue she reserved for these stale hours at home.

When she had finished sweeping, she turned to face him, shards of glass glimmering in the dustpan.

The old woman looked up at him too. Her eyes were dull and indifferent, as if they had been carved out of a lustreless rock. Then he thought he caught a glint of viciousness in them. And the smell hit him again, a heavy slug of sulphur.

He backed out of the room, mumbling an apology, and went down the stairs two at a time.

He parked the car opposite the lake. All around him, the wind shook the tops of trees. He tried her number again as he sat in the car, staring at the dark waters, now beginning to swell and roll. He began and abandoned a text message. It was the first time in his life that words held themselves beyond his grasp. The sky continued to darken, great black wings of cloud coasting in from every direction. Two skiffs from the Calcutta Rowing Club pitched to one side in the middle of the lake and then struggled back to the jetty. When the first drops began to drum gently on the roof of the car, he leaned his head back and waited for them to beat down.

'I brought some peaches.'

She looked at the bag in his hands.

'From Spain. You said that she liked soft fruit.'

She stepped back from the door, a hateful look on her face, as if in spite of her best efforts she admitted defeat.

The old couple were sitting exactly as before. Clothes were heaped on one of the sofas and the smell of detergent had broken through the old odours. A window was banging against its pane in one of the bedrooms and she rushed to close it. He remained standing in the middle of the room, and the couple took no notice of him.

She answered a call from the hospital, about a mix-up over some test results, and then another call, one that seemed to only add to the confusion. There was the sound of a bucket being filled with water; then the pressure cooker let out a sharp whistle.

She walked past him as if he were inanimate, like one of the heavy pieces of furniture in the room. He could see into one of the bedrooms. A fancy sari hung from a wardrobe handle, covered in the plastic from the dry cleaners. For a moment he thought she might be preparing to go out and then he realized that the sari had probably hung there for many weeks, many months.

The old woman began to cough, a loud sound that seemed to echo around the room. Her husband shot her a baleful look and returned to his contemplations.

She stopped what she was doing to rub her mother's back.

'Look up, Ma, look up,' she said in an unfamiliar voice, low and mild.

She stood on a stool and reached for a box on one of the high shelves. Her body seemed suspended in that instant, and he knew that this would be the image of her he would carry for the rest of his life: the stretch of her arms in a corner of this bleak room, the place where her ardour arose, the point from which she created different versions of herself.

Someone yelled from the car park that the new gas cylinder had arrived and she hurried downstairs.

He wondered who stayed with the couple when she was out, out with him. Moving closer to the table, he smiled at the old man, who instantly looked away. He did not know whether he ought to ask them if they wanted anything. As a rule, he never asked questions when he was not likely to receive a response; that was why he never talked to infants or animals. But the silence was oppressive: it swelled and sneered.

'She'll be back in a minute,' he said.

There was no reaction from the old woman's eyes; they continued to stare.

The old man had shifted his gaze to the glass doors. A magpie had flown onto the balcony and was studying a string of wooden birds that hung from a hook in the ceiling. It shook its head and hopped along the railing. Then it flew up to one of the birds and gave it a hopeful sort of peck. The old man nodded in encouragement.

'Can I get you something?' he asked the old man.

'Some water?'

He noticed that there was a glass of water on the table.

It had been a while since she had gone downstairs. A panicked thought crossed his mind for an instant that she had seized the opportunity and disappeared for good, leaving him to cope with the old couple.

There was the sound that he had heard before – the little whimper.

'Are you hungry, Auntie?' he asked.

They both stared at him.

He walked into the kitchen. He looked on the counter top for the peaches, opened the fridge door with a rare timidity and then glanced into the bin in the corner. They were nowhere to be seen.

There was a pan on the hob. He lifted its lid and felt a starchy punch of steam on his face. The soup was a mellow green and it smelt of an unidentifiable herb.

'I brought some peaches but I can't find them,' he said to the other room.

He turned around to face a row of transparent jars on a shelf – there was salt in the jar marked 'coffee'.

'Will you have some soup?' he asked.

He found a bowl on a rack above the hob and ladled some soup into it, pouring half of it back into the pan. Blowing into the bowl, he took it to the old lady.

'It smells delicious,' he said.

He put the bowl down on the table in front of her. She peered into it with interest and then a little misgiving. She blinked.

Sitting down opposite her, he held a spoonful of soup in front of her lips.

She glanced at the spoon and then looked at him with confusion.

He blew on the spoon.

'It's soup,' he said.

As if on cue, her jaw dropped down and she leaned forward.

'So, you were hungry,' he said.

She swallowed and opened her mouth again, far wider than was strictly necessary.

He gave her another spoonful.

She appeared to like it. Of course, it was possible that she thought it was some sort of soft fruit.

Behind her, he could see bookcase doors with glass knobs, deep ridges cut into their surface, designed by someone with no heed for the grime that could accumulate there. On the middle shelf there was a fat volume with familiar black and white lettering on its spine. He too owned a copy of that book, a history of Burma, one that he had picked up more than fifteen years ago and slotted in a corner of his study, where it remained, unread. Seeing the book here, he felt a little flip in his chest.

He gave her a few more spoons and then, taking his handkerchief out of his pocket, wiped a dribble on her chin.

'It's tasty, isn't it?' he said, as she ran her tongue around her mouth.

Her husband watched her eat, a slight wash of pride on his face. He could have been watching his daughter perform in a school play. Then he turned to look at the string of wooden birds on the balcony. The magpie had gone.

He wondered which of them would die first. It would be a relief, a tragedy, perhaps the shattering of an integral symmetry.

'One more spoon,' he said, holding it out.

She swallowed and let out a delicate burp.

He glanced down at the bowl. There was only a splash or so left.

SUZIE BABY

Murders: forty-seven. Kidnappings: fourteen. Attempted rapes: five. Car chases: fourteen. Hijacks: two. Helicopter jumps: one. Smuggling expeditions: countless.

It's not exactly Sir Laurence Olivier. But in summing up my film career, mendacity will serve no one. I have acted in eleven films, three of which were shelved: two for financial reasons, the third as a result of the producer's conviction in a racketeering case. Of the eight releases, two were declared super hits, two did average business and the rest were wholly rejected by the masses.

These days, I have opted for a simple life, free from the trilling of the film world. But I continue to be connected to my métier through my acting academy, where I give classes four days a week. The location, one of the studios of an unkempt gym in Jogeshwari, is not ideal. It is, however, quite close to my home, the rent is reasonable, and I am able to occupy the room at non-peak hours when the din of the aerobics classes is only an unpleasant memory.

Abhay has been training at my academy for just under a year. He is twenty-six and pleasant. He has a hard, athletic body over which he lavishes much care, and a singularly naïve face. The overall impression he gives is that of a calf in a tight T-shirt. Over the last few weeks, he has desecrated numerous iconic monologues, misunderstood almost every aspect of improvisation and, with the assistance of four fellow students, enacted a ghastly comedy routine. He also sings, although thankfully not at me.

Abhay tells me that he has reached a crucial point in his journey. A few weeks ago, his regular attendance outside the office of a prominent producer finally yielded a result. He was allowed into the sanctum sanctorum to meet the great man. His photographs were accepted and I have no doubt that his journey was discussed. A week or so later, quite surprisingly, he was summoned to the producer's offices again, where he met a few more notable personalities, I forget whom. The following day, he was asked to do a screen test. There may have been other readings and run-throughs. With all this background activity, he stopped attending classes. I said nothing of it.

It is not my concern whether they show up or not. Drag a horse to water and so forth.

Yesterday, Abhay turned up just as my class was ending. He wanted to have a private word. He told me that discussions with the film producer had reached an advanced stage. It was 95 per cent guaranteed that he had secured the role of the second lead in a big banner film. The producer's assistant had informed Abhay that a decision was imminent and that he would be telephoned around four the next afternoon.

I congratulated Abhay. I told him that I had always believed that his capability and dedication would bring him the success he deserved. He had tears in his eyes. It could have been the emotions of the past few days or maybe he really does have some acting talent.

As I was preparing to leave the room, he fell to the ground and tried to touch my feet. Naturally, I recoiled. He had one more thing to ask me, he said. Would I please wait with him the following afternoon when the call from the producer's office was due? I was, he said, like a father to him and he believed I would bring him good luck. I may have ordered an elderly invalid to be torn apart by wild dogs in one of my films, but I am not a monster. I could hardly refuse with the boy trembling at my feet like a TB patient. Just this once I decided to indulge poor, witless Abhay.

And so I find myself sitting here with him in a cheap restaurant, a place that he assured me would be empty at this time. Naturally it is not, and from time to time all we can hear is the sound of waiters bellowing their orders to the kitchen.

And in any case, there will be no call. There will be no second-lead role. There will be no big banner film; at least, not for Abhay. I am not sure if Bombay film producers are congenitally sadistic or whether boredom drives them to these acts. What I do know is that there have been innumerable instances of firm promises, accompanied by a ceremony of meritocratic selection, none of which has resulted in so much as a walk-on part in a horror film. I have seen it happen time and time again. I suppose I should feel sorry for Abhay, but if he still has not learnt these basic facts, he probably deserves the thrashing he is due to get.

He seems oblivious to the fact that we are only a couple of feet away from the bedlam of the Jogeshwari–Vikhroli Link Road. Bombay has changed immeasurably. For one thing, we are encouraged to call it Mumbai. The JVLR is now a multi-lane colossus that apparently makes life much easier for commuters. That is for others to comment on since I no longer drive and my life takes me no further from Andheri than Jogeshwari. The property prices, the pollution, the policing: all changes very dear to the hearts of the bourgeois occupants of my building, but of little interest to me.

There is a certain pleasure in teaching these youngsters, regardless of the fact that most are no better than chimps swinging in a zoo. I coach acting as science: psychology, physics and anatomy. I provide sessions in body language, expressions, voice modulation and character deconstruction. There are practical aspects too, such as camera angles and the pitfalls of auditions. I do not teach fighting or dancing. They can easily learn that elsewhere. Some of them are disappointed when they discover that action sequences will not be on the curriculum. Given my past, they probably arrived here thinking it would be the most prominent area of instruction.

I did not set out to hold sway as one of Hindi cinema's most barbarous villains. Like many of my colleagues who found themselves looting temples and silencing informants, I ventured into the film industry hoping to be cast in romantic lead roles. It is true that someone of my elite drama school training would have been expected to have a natural inclination for the stage. But I was convinced that I could add a dash of refinement to the mainstream medium, expunging its gaudiest strokes. I spent years supplicating and genuflecting, trying to melt hearts and set fire to loins. It was not to be. I was routinely ignored, insulted or dismissed. Nevertheless, I was lucky. Unlike most actors, I had both ambition and insight. In time I came to see that my imposing stature and patrician mien could be assets in the field of cinematic depravity.

It seems strange to recall those times in this restaurant, surrounded by various employees of a nearby hospital, identifiable by the grubby passes they are still sporting around their necks. There are so many streaks and scratches on the laminated surface of the menu that it looks like a piece of frosted glass. Abhay could at least have picked a place with air conditioning. It is October, Bombay's second summer, and my shirt is beginning to stick to my back even though I am not normally given to extravagant perspiration. This was always an advantage when I used to film. Shooting under studio lights, or on a scorching airfield runway, or sometimes in the humidity of Madh Island, I was able to perform take after take with little or no retouching by the make-up assistant. No mean feat when one considers that I would probably have been in a wide-lapelled cream sports jacket or a three-piece suit.

My first and biggest success was *Dushman ka Khoon* (1976). I spotted recently on several websites that the title has been translated into English as *The Enemy's Blood*; I think 'Enemy Blood', eschewing the definitive article and the possessive form, would have been more elegant. I understand also that a DVD version of the film is circulating in Southall and other ethnic localities of British cities with the subtitle *Sinister Revenge*. No doubt those in charge know what they are doing.

Details of the denouement are unnecessary: suffice it to say that I was endowed, in this film, with a glass eye, an underwater hideout and a leopard on a leash. The vamp assigned to me was initially called Maria. But in the course of filming, the character's name was changed to Suzie, with its frisson of promiscuity.

And that brings me to what has perhaps become my most important legacy in Indian popular culture: the phrase that is still occasionally shouted at me from taxis and construction sites.

'Suzie baby, why don't you come a little closer?'

The line had initially been conceptualized in Hindi, 'Suzie baby, zara paas aake baitho na', but it was felt that my delivery of the words in English achieved a more precise lewdness. I remember clearly the day that we filmed the scene. I had rehearsed the line in Hindi a couple of times and the director, Murad Khan, remained unconvinced. There was something about the purity of my intonation that did not accord with the revolving bed on which I sat. It occurred to me that a simple switch to English might solve the problem. So not only did I deliver the line, in a small way I was also responsible for its creation.

There are those who continue to carp that we simply copied the other popular catchphrase of the era: 'Mona darling'. I concede that there is a degree of semblance. This line too was uttered in a number of films by a celebrated villain of the seventies, Ajit, to his scantily clad female sidekick. Like me, Ajit represented the more polished criminal, a blackguard with class. But any similarities must end there. For one thing, he was a good many years older than me. He also possessed an acting style that was antithetic to mine, favouring a rather broad and conspicuous projection.

In terms of the line itself, taken in context, there is a world of difference between 'Suzie baby' and 'Mona darling'. A proper elucidation would require a forensic enquiry into the plots of our various films, so I will only repeat what was once said by Jean-Luc Godard: 'Cinema is not an art that films life; it is something between art and life.'

Suzie was played by a young actress called Sulochana Ganapathy. Her family was originally from Hassan in Karnataka, but having grown up in Lucknow, she spoke the most elegant Hindi. It was unfortunate that most of her negligible lines were in English. Her name was considered inappropriate for a siren, so she was given the screen name Roshni Rani. I doubt whether she had any say in the matter.

Sulochana had a strange, disorderly beauty on screen. Her face was a little elongated, her eyes tended to look surprised and she could bring a nuanced tremble to her bottom lip, barely perceptible to the naked eye. I suppose that these days she would be considered somewhat full-figured. Then she was thought to have a very covetable shape, all snap and sway. She was a classically trained dancer, Bharatanatyam, I believe. In *Dushman ka Khoon* she made her entrance sliding down a chute into a tub of foam.

I met Sulochana on the first day of filming. She had been living some sort of hand-to-mouth existence as a junior artist, her unfortunate tale no different from all those other thousands. Her experiences had already given her face the expression much seen in the Bombay film world: part earnest, part craven. That film was her break, as it was mine. Although to witness our brief conversations in between shots, anyone would have thought that I was already a huge star. She deferred to everything I said, no matter how desultory. She asked me endless questions about her expressions, her poise and her accent. I was probably quite dismissive. She irritated me. What had poise got to do with sprawling half-naked on a mound of fake bank notes?

Sulochana was cast as my chief moll in two further films. Producers must have appreciated a certain celluloid chemistry between us. Either as some form of branding or out of creative sloth, her character's name remained Suzie in both films. It seemed inevitable then that my much-appreciated line from *Dushman ka Khoon* would be repeated a number of times whenever we shared the screen. I think I spent a good part of the late seventies encouraging Sulochana to come a little closer.

By chance, I saw Sulochana about ten years ago. She must have been in her early fifties then. It was the first time that we had seen each other since dubbing for the last film we did together in 1979. The occasion was not a happy one. It was the fourteenth-day ceremony of Vishal Patil, a character actor who had shown me a number of kindnesses in my days as a novice. He had succumbed to a heart attack and, being well liked in the industry, had attracted a large gathering of mourners.

I was taken aback to see Sulochana there. I had heard that she had married and left Bombay. She seemed genuinely pleased to see me. I am not sure why that should have surprised me, but it did. She looked content.

Her face was fuller and her hair was cut short. She told me that she had married a businessman who manufactured something in Pune and that she had two children. She mentioned a few people that we had both known, either to enquire after their well-being or to say that she had run into them. Neither of us brought up our work together. As I left, she was talking to Vishal's son. I was pleased to see that she was still able to bring that tremble to her bottom lip.

I look at Abhay over the top of my glasses: all of a sudden, he is a virtuoso in high drama. In class he often finds it difficult to entice a discernible emotion into his repertoire, but today, I see a superlative execution of muttering, grimacing and entreating. My tea is sugary and the colour of rust. It is a quarter to four.

It takes some effort but I try to focus on Abhay, even though I am in a damp shirt, seated at a table in this lousy restaurant, waiting for a phone call that will never come. He begins to speak again of the film, news of which is so eagerly being anticipated this afternoon. It involves an airline tycoon, several mistaken identities and a comedy kidnapping. The outdoor shooting schedules have been fixed in the US, South Africa and Thailand. The main lead is the scion of an acting dynasty who is proving to be very popular, despite looking like a lethargic ape. There are a string of heroines, none of whose names I care to remember but all of the same breed: nonentities who enjoy shrieking at their own taut stomachs.

None of my former or current students have enjoyed anything that could be termed a success. One or two may have made it on to a crowd scene in a television serial. These days, there are only three feasible routes for actors in Bombay. One needs to be a close relative of powerful industry players; one is foisted on to some unfortunate producer by a criminal with clout; or one possesses incomparable skills in providing sexual favours to the people who matter. Needless to say, I do not spell this out to my apprentices. If they are not able to arrive at these conclusions without assistance, they are even greater imbeciles than I imagined. We will continue with diction and close-up camera skills until they see the light.

It is one minute to four. The call is due any time now. I wonder how long I will be expected to commiserate and fortify. I had planned on drawing the curtains and settling down with a drink this afternoon to watch *The Third Man* again. It is one of my favourites, an irrefutable classic. Orson Welles brings a special intensity to the character of Harry Lime, adrift in decadent post-war Vienna. I do feel that at one or two points his phrasing becomes sluggish, diminishing the amoral force of the character. But, all in all, a very creditable performance. Notwithstanding the relatively modest screen time, I believe that it was a role I was born to play.

Since the release of my final film, on the professional front my life has been relatively quiet. In the mid-nineties I was cast in a television serial as the family patriarch, a college professor with high ideals. The show bombed. I was told that audiences were unable to accept that I would be the type of man who railed against institutional corruption while monitoring the social lives of his unwed daughters. All appearances to the contrary, it seemed that the image of my character pushing a terrified mother into a pool of lava in *Mera Badla* (1977) was fresh in the nation's consciousness. I reacted with grace, shouldered the blame for the show's failure, and heaped praise on the writers and junior actors, most of whom would not recognize a three-dimensional character even if it ran them down in a BEST bus.

In subsequent years, I entered the fray a couple more times, taking on tedious roles in serials with unimpressive runs. In 1999, I appeared on the small screen again in a public service film with an anti-smoking message. I played an obstinate smoker who croaked his regrets from his deathbed, while his family wept around him passionately. After that, no narrations I heard suited me, no ideas inspired me. The truth is that Hindi cinema can no longer accommodate the exemplar of a monumental villain. Today, the gangsters are all lovable losers, the avaricious industrialists are being feted and, following the economic reforms of Dr Manmohan Singh in the nineties, the smuggler has become extinct.

An actor's life: the waxing and waning of a particular kind of moon. I am fortunate that in my fecund years I purchased outright a splendid apartment in Andheri. Some twenty years ago, on my mother's passing, I also inherited her Dadar home. These factors have combined to ensure that I am financially secure and do not need to depend on the good offices of film and television producers for my subsistence. The desire to perform, however, never really retreats.

Abhay is staring at his phone. It is a quarter past four. I am tiring of this game. I appreciate that this is the closest he has ever come to seeing something of worth in his life. He thinks it is a pivotal moment. As he sips his fresh lime soda, I can see that the forces of destiny, or whatever he calls it, have etched themselves on to his forehead. I motion to a waiter to turn the fan up.

It is twenty past four. I open my mouth to tell Abhay that I have to leave. He interjects first. He apologizes and tells me that the call should be coming any time now: of course, someone with my experience knows what these film-wallahs are like. He is very sorry for the delay and asks me if I would like another cup of tea. I would not. I decide to give him five more minutes.

I wonder whether he will continue to present himself at producers' offices tomorrow onwards, memorize dialogue from well-known scenes to perform at auditions, do five hundred press-ups a day. There must be a moment of epiphany even for someone as blinkered as Abhay, a day of violent adjustment, a repositioning towards fitness trainer, salesman or driver. He is still staring at his phone, a bead of sweat settled in his cupid's bow, willing the call to come. Drilling equipment has been set in motion outside the restaurant – more cacophony to add to this already pitiful scene.

I motion for the bill. Abhay pretends that he did not see, and is playing with a string tied around his wrist. The drilling gets louder and then stops.

The phone rings.

Abhay looks at me, terrified. I nod in reassurance. At least I will be able to go home soon. He answers the phone, swinging around in his seat, away from me, his back hunched into the conversation. He says 'yes, sir' and 'thank you, sir' a few times. I wonder if I will get stuck in any traffic on my way back.

Abhay straightens up and puts the phone down on the table. He has tears in his eyes again.

He has got the part.

He has to report to them on the following day and they will begin settling the details, the signing amount, dates and so forth. The waiter brings the bill.

I give Abhay my hand and congratulate him. I tell him that I have always believed that his capability and dedication would bring him the success he deserves. He is crying openly now. People will think he is my wayward son or a gigolo. I stand up and motion to the door, leaving him to pay the bill.

Outside, I stop a taxi. Abhay emerges and thanks me again for everything that I have done. He insists that he wants to accompany me to my door; it is, he says, his duty. I tell him that it is out of his way, he has much to organize and not to trouble himself. I will be fine, I say.

I get into the taxi and leave.

Even though it is not far, the journey to my place seems endless. The heat is exhausting and my shirt is now soaked. Fumes are everywhere, and by the time I get out of the taxi, I have a sore throat. The driver claims he does not have change so I tell him that he will get five rupees less than the fare.

I take the lift to the fifth floor and return to my flat. I pour myself a whisky; some of it sloshes on to my wrist. I slam the freezer door because the ice trays are empty. My drink tastes like warm ash so I push it away. My mobile phone rings. It is Abhay. I ignore it. He sends me a convoluted text message. He has already begun arranging a party to celebrate his role. It will probably be at a hotel in Oshiwara tomorrow evening as he has to leave for Cape Town as soon as his visa is ready. I switch off my phone. As I walk back to the kitchen, I see an envelope on the floor, pushed under the front door. I must have missed it when I came in. I pick it up and rip out the card. It is an invitation to the wedding anniversary function of one of the couples who inhabit my building. I tear it into little pieces and then fling them over the balcony. Hands on the balustrade, I watch them as they fall.

A lorry swerved to avoid a herd of goats outside the cotton mandi and careered off the road, pitching its load of metal rods in three directions. One stave pierced the stomach of a goat and it bolted into the bazaar, crazed with pain and fear. It dashed from one mound of cotton to another, jets of blood spattering the pristine lint and smearing across the stone floor. A good ten minutes of clamour and curses passed before the goat was caught and its sagging entrails jammed back into its body. The day's business was ruined. Furious traders flung the animal into a ditch where it came to a shuddering end and thrashed the lorry driver until he lost consciousness.

Across the road from the market's main entrance, a face on a poster watched the ugly scene. It fluttered and flapped and finally sailed to the ground as the wind tore it loose from an electricity pole. The face whirled down the lane in short bursts, over the verge and far into a field. But it was not out of sight. The same face was plastered on boundary walls and water tanks. It stared from pink leaflets that were slipped under doors and flung into courtyards. A cycle rickshaw outside the post office was festooned with its features. The face was crumpled up, ripped up, rolled up and used as kindling. The captions were different: 'YOU ARE NOT ALONE,' or 'YESU SAVES' or 'CHRIST IS THE CURE'; but the face was the same.

Most of the villagers immediately recognized it as Upkaar's wife. The woman had abandoned him and disappeared some years ago – transforming him from a creature of no consequence to a kinsman who deserved every sympathy. There had been vicious talk for a while, but after a year or so, it was quickly settled that she must be given up for dead. Now, as they stared with astonishment at her face, they stamped their feet in the early morning fog, breathed into their fists and rubbed their arms for warmth. Of course, there was loud speculation about her return as a messenger for a different god. But there was also a murky apprehension of her new prominence, doubts that were only voiced in private.

Upkaar picked at the corner of a poster and pulled it free of the tree trunk. The features were unmistakable: the face still lean, the pale lips creased in concentration, the irises blacker than anything else on the page. He balled up the paper, crammed it into his pocket and made his way home.

When he heard his name wheezed from a point behind him, somewhere among the sacks of millet and the bags of seed, he kept walking. When the call was repeated, his strides lengthened, his eyes fixed on the ground. As he turned into the dirt track at the edge of the village, he was determined not to glance back. The men piling the fodder into hummocks had lowered their forks as he walked past. Heads had bobbed at the sath under the banyan tree, but not in greeting. That was no ordinary look from Charan Tayiji as she parched maize in her usual spot, her spoon hitting the side of the karhai with an inquisitive clank.

He pushed against his front door with the heel of his palm and locked it behind him. Fallen leaves, furled into dry spindles, lay strewn across the courtyard. A lizard on the brickwork above the door darted from sunlight into shadow. He sat on the charpoy and waited for the knock. It came a few minutes later.

Manjeet greeted him with a clap on the shoulder and eyebrows raised in a simulacrum of affection.

'You have become very hard to catch these days,' he said.

Upkaar shut the door and locked it again.

'You come and go like smoke,' said Manjeet, a spot of light gleaming on the tip of his nose.

Manjeet searched his face for a sign of thaw but found only the same frigid features. Jamming his hands into the pockets of his kurta, he looked around at the unswept courtyard.

'It doesn't matter how many times I have said it, I will say it one more time. You should have got married again,' he said.

It was a perfect segue.

'And that reminds me, how could I have forgotten to ask you, have you seen the posters?'

'No,' said Upkaar.

'They are on the walls by the shop,' he added. 'What a sight, first thing in the morning. Who would believe it?'

'I don't want to hear any more,' said Upkaar.

'No need to be like that. Here a man comes to find out how you are, tell you which way the wind is blowing and you can't even show a little interest,' said Manjeet, drawing his shawl tighter around him.

He glanced once more with distaste around the courtyard – a pile of dirty clothes on the charpoy, the blackened pots abandoned in a corner.

As he walked out the door, he turned his head and said: 'You know, I really don't understand why you didn't get married again.'

Upkaar turned to lock the door again, smiling wryly at the thought of another wife. He had gone far enough with the one he had. They had throbbed and rasped and jangled in this courtyard, until she packed a small bag and left the house one grey dawn. And where would this new wife come from? Even the young men of the village could not find brides in the surrounding areas. Hardly any girls had been born here for decades, wrenched from their mothers' wombs when their sex was discovered. Cash changed hands all over these parts for wives from Bengal, Bihar, even distant Kerala.

It was a miracle that he had even married once, that a family had been prepared to give him their daughter. Everyone knew about his bad blood and its strains of madness. His uncle had lost his mind and walked into the torrents of a river swollen by the monsoon. A year later, his father had tottered from eccentricity into insanity. He began to speak tearfully of non-existent relatives and hid dirty rags behind loose bricks in the kitchen wall. Several times he made his way to the station at Ferozepur, convinced that if he laid his head on the rail tracks, he would receive messages from the other side of the border, reports on plans for reunification, instructions for his family and friends. In the end, Upkaar's mother tied him to a post in the courtyard and dozed on her knees next to him, in case he tried to pull himself free in the night.

Upkaar pushed the clothes off the charpoy, dragged it into the shade and lay down, his hands clasped behind his head, the bulge of paper in his pocket burning into him like hot coal. He thought once more of her dark irises. He turned over on to his side and the image turned to lie with him.

Upkaar stood in line at the ironsmith, his head wrapped in a muffler, his limbs drawn inwards. The two waiting men had their backs to him.

'Have you heard? In Amrika, or was it Japan, they are trying to put a pig's heart inside a man.'

'What for?'

'Idiot, his own heart stopped working, why else?'

'What kind of life would that be, wandering around with the heart of a pig? Just think, when you are lying on top of a woman, what she can hear is a pig's heartbeat.'

'Dhak-dhak, dhak-dhak.'

'Better to die with no heart.'

'Take care, my friend. All that liquor you put down your throat. That could be you going to hospital with the pig.'

'It's you who will get that pig's heart, khusra.'

'Why?'

'To match your face.'

The men stopped talking when they glimpsed Upkaar.

He could tell that the men wanted to know, more than anything, whether he would be going to the prayer meeting. What face did a man wear to hear his estranged wife speak of the mysteries of Christ?

The prayer meeting was to take place in an empty field, on the banks of a stream, fifteen kilometres from the village. Some of the people there would have already welcomed Jesus into their lives and would revel in that sanctuary. There would be waverers: shaky, cowed, irresolute. The incensed would go, swallowing their outrage at the proselytization in order to take careful note of what was said and who was there. Others would be unable to resist the opportunity to witness the spectacle of a woman who had left the village in disgrace and then returned as a divine agent. And a few would attend because it was a quiet part of the world and they turned up to anything held in a tent.

Upkaar would not be going.

He did not want to hear praises sung of any god, least of all by her. He would not be a witness to her ornate rebirth. If she wanted to see him, she could come to the house she had left and find him there. There had to be pardon and penance in the religion that she preached: she would have to come to him to seek them.

He had always been convinced that she would return. It was a knowledge that he had kept hidden, knowing it would be ridiculed if ever discovered. It was like a quiet but tenacious belief in the earth being flat, in spite of the wealth of photographs, maps and globes that proclaimed otherwise. Fields rippled in green and gold to the land's irrefutable edge; rivers flowed across plains that found themselves suddenly caught short; the horizon was its own final word. He knew what he knew. Kamal would make her way back to the village one day.

They married each other because there was no reason to object to the marriage. Kamal brought hardly any possessions and only one photograph, a picture of a mountain lake that she could not possibly have visited. There were things about her that surprised him: she sang through the day, her voice curiously cracked and hoarse for a young woman; she showed no qualm when it came to slaughter and would wring a chicken's neck as if it were a wad of washing; when he first pressed his fingers into her calf, he encountered a thick ridge of muscle. They tried for a child, pitching and sweating on the charpoy, on the courtyard floor, upright against the locked door. Every day the drift of soot from the chulha crept up the wall, inch by inch.

When Kamal was seven months' pregnant, the skin on her stomach already looked as if it was stretched to the limit, its gloss a warning. She had been running a fever on and off for a few days but it had been hard to tell that summer, when heat devoured everything without and within. She was standing in the doorway when she lost the baby, her palms pressing into the jambs. By the time Upkaar rushed home from the fields it was all over. The women had left and she was cocooned in a blanket in an airless corner of the house, her lips dry and splitting. One spot of blood remained on the sill of the doorway.

Charan Tayijee said that it was just as well since it had been a girl.

After that, Kamal stopped singing and nothing had ever sounded as silent as that absence of song. Upkaar said that they should try again, they should never stop trying, and put his hand on her thigh. She slapped it away. He ran his fingers through the fat coil of her hair, his fist forming hard.

'It was your cursed blood that did it,' she said.

He struck her across the face and pushed her down, driven by an urge somewhere between lust and rage. She fought back, clawing at his chest, biting his jaw, slamming her feet into his groin. He backed away, his chest heaving. She swore that if he ever came near her again she would cut his throat while he slept.

She developed a fascination for all the aberrant occurrences of this world: the rapes, the murders, the horrific accidents on highways. It was as if constant talk of the morbid newspaper reports would sweep away the casts of her anger. Upkaar tried to reason with her, inveigle her, then to diminish her. He came up behind her and tried to slide his arms around her waist. She walked away, reached for a blanket and went up to sleep on the roof.

Every evening he watched her standing in the doorway, looking out into the darkness of the fields. Her head was cocked and alert. This was a place where boulders rolled down hills in the dead of night, where tractors burst into flames, where poisoned water swirled and slapped against the sides of wells, where foxes ate their young.

It was a neighbour who brought Brother Rajan into their lives. He walked into the courtyard with timid steps, a man of discretion and patience, under his arm a document carrier that looked as if it was polished on the hour. The glare of the sunlight on Brother Rajan's glasses gave him a baffled but delighted look, as if he had not expected to be in such company, but now that he had arrived there was no other place he would rather be. Kamal was a different woman, covering her head, urging more and more tea on him, giving the document carrier its own seat.

'There is no pressure,' said Brother Rajan, blowing at his tea. 'All I request you to do is to come once and see if it does not bring some peace to your heart.'

His Punjabi was slow, soft and heavily accented, and where the appropriate word escaped him, he stuck out the tip of his tongue and plucked an alternative in Hindi or English or Tamil.

He raised his index finger.

'But please, one more request. Don't talk about the church here, there and everywhere. If you have friends and neighbours who might want to come, who need to be unburdened, I welcome them with all my heart. But otherwise, too much talk, too much show, it can make people here angry. We have to proceed slowly.'

Upkaar wanted to snap Brother Rajan's glasses in two and fling him into the dirt road. If one religion had failed them, leaving only the dry husks of ritual, Upkaar did not intend beginning afresh with another.

The temporary church was the home of Mangal Lal, a cotton trader whose canny land deals had allowed a number of refurbishments and extensions, making his house one of the largest in the village. There were few other circumstances in which Upkaar and Kamal could have expected to find themselves there. Kamal had chosen to wear the salwar kameez that she had worn on the day of her wedding. Upkaar had left his face unwashed.

They were welcomed into the house by Mangal's wife, Poonam.

'Welcome to the house of Yesu,' she said.

A dozen or so worshippers had gathered on quilts and rugs in the centre of the room. Brother Rajan faced the group, his index finger in the air. Kamal squatted as close to him as possible, squeezing into the small space between two women in the first row.

'Yesu loves and forgives and is always ready to welcome you, no matter what mistakes you have made, no matter how low you think you have been born. In this church, we are all equal,' he said.

A poster of Christ surrounded by lambs, cherubs and blonde-mopped children was reflected in the large television screen behind Brother Rajan. Smiling at Kamal, he continued: 'We can build schools to educate your children, give you medicine when you are sick, food when you are hungry, we have kind and generous friends in places all over the world. But remember, this is only because of the grace of Yesu Masih.'

'How many have come over this week?' asked Mangal Lal, seated next to Brother Rajan like a deputy.

'Forty-four just in this district,' said Brother Rajan.

He turned to his audience again.

'Opening your heart to Yesu Prabhu is just like cooking for a feast, preparing langar for all. We must do it together. Brother Sandeep brings the wheat, Brother Pritpal mills it fine, Sister Simran has drawn water and brought oil, Sister Parminder kneads the dough and rolls out the rotis, I will cook them on the tawa until they are done. In the same way, we each bring what we can into this church:

honesty, grace, devotion, prayers; and we create peace and love for all,' he said.

Upkaar shifted in his seat in the back of the room and massaged his toes, one after another.

'Now,' said Brother Rajan, clapping his hands.

One of the women began to pump at her harmonium and next to her the dhol started up.

'With your heart wide open,' squealed Brother Rajan.

It was a familiar song but with the words altered. Instead of eyes lined with kohl and bangles clinking on wrists, the song now spoke of a wandering man who found the path to Yesu Prabhu. Far from bells and domes and ghats, they sang in front of the cross on the coffee table, with each note clambering further into the vision laid before them by Brother Rajan, having wrested their future from one god and promised it to another.

Upkaar watched Brother Rajan closely, searching for signs of frailty or deception.

But Brother Rajan was earnest and unshakable, clapping his hands in time to the dhol as the light glanced off his glasses.

On their way home, Upkaar broke the silence.

'Did you hear what he said? About the money that will come from his foreign friends?'

'So?'

'So you people are not worshipping Yesu. Your new god is some rich, fat man in Amrika who is sending your Brother Rajan plenty of dollars to buy you all.'

'No one asked you to come. You should have stayed at home.'

'And that song that you were all singing so happily to praise Yesu? That is our song, a song of Punjab, every child knows that song. They have just changed the words to fool idiots like you.'

Kamal walked on ahead, the sequins in her chunni catching the beam from Upkaar's torch.

The next morning when he woke, she had already left the house. He didn't spot her again until he was on his way back from the fields that afternoon. She and two others were standing waist deep in the trough next to a tube well, their baptism complete. She followed him home, her clothes soaked, her hair falling in damp twists over her shoulders. When Upkaar reached for a bucket to wash the dirt from the fields off his feet, she began to croon the song from the night before, repeating the chorus over and over in her ragged tones. Then she went to the roof to hang her chunni up to dry. As it flapped in the wind, she sat down on her haunches, her face turned upwards, still singing.

He decided to go to the prayer meeting after all. He walked in spite of the sun. It would give him time to vanquish the troubling images in his mind: Kamal making her way through a crowd, acknowledging bows with a restrained nod of her own; Kamal standing on a stage, holding a mike with both hands; Kamal and Brother Rajan deep in prayer. He pulled down a low hanging branch, broke off a limb, stripped it of its leaves and made himself a staff.

He took the canal path, keeping an eye on the road across the fields where tractors, carts and lorries trickled in the direction he was headed. The chug and rumble of tube wells filled the air as he walked through thickets of mango trees and past clumps of bhekar, sticky with sap. He slashed at shrubs and grasses with his staff, lopping off any seed heads he could reach. He had begun to enjoy the rhythm of his walk and had almost forgotten his destination.

On the lower ground ahead, he could see the top of the tent, yellow swirls on a red background. He threw his staff into the canal and enjoyed the dull plop it made. The cracks and swishes of his tread meant that he did not hear the footsteps until they were almost at his heels. He felt a hand on his shoulder and turned around.

The man who had stopped him appeared to be from some nether world. His skin looked like the rind of an abominable fruit and his hair stood in wild tufts. One of his eyes threatened to leap out of its nest of angry capillaries, the other was inert and almost closed. The stench that came from his mouth could have been liquor, disease or death.

'A few rupees,' said the man, his good eye settling on the ground between them.

'What?' mumbled Upkaar, taking a step back.

'Just what you have,' said the man.

The air thickened and pressed against Upkaar's face. The man's head lolled as if the bhukki in his veins was just beginning to take effect.

Upkaar took another step back.

'Whatever you have,' said the man, his good eye journeying up to meet Upkaar's gaze.

Dozens of gnats appeared between them, sweeping in from the canal, flittering and thrumming, moving from shape to shape in an instant.

The man grabbed Upkaar's wrist and felt for a watch. It was only then that Upkaar noticed the bicycle pump he grasped in his fist. The black cylinder reared up in a blur and caught Upkaar between the eyes. He reeled to one side and only collapsed when the metal cracked into his skull for a second time.

When he was sure that his eyes were open, he saw the pale bowl of the sky. The top of his head felt as though it had turned soft and fleshy, like the crown of a newborn, and there was a pain that could have been anywhere, his mouth, his eyes, his shins. He touched his face to feel the shell that had hardened over it: his own bad blood. There was no sign of the man.

The sound of applause burst through, across the fields and on to this pitted path by the canal. A deep voice boomed and cracked over the speaker system and there was more applause. Then a voice. He could not recognize it, distorted by separation, sweep and exposure. But it had to be her. The lean face with the dark irises, the pastorni was speaking. He held his breath, trying to make out the words.

'We were trapped in a cave and then, one day, the rock was rolled away and light came flooding in. Do not condemn your soul to eternal damnation, to the most excruciating pain, the most unbearable grief, the most terrible hunger.'

A laugh began to purl its way up from deep in his belly. It squeezed its way around his chest, tickled his tongue and sputtered into a snicker on his lips. He took a breath and let it out as a muddy gurgle. His face collapsed into itself and his shoulders shook.

'Open your eyes, open your heart; that is all you have to do and let the love of Masih flood in.'

He unclenched his fists, engulfed by gasps and snorts and yawps.

'It is never too late to save yourselves and the ones that are most dear to you.'

His ribs seemed to shift as he breathed in. And still the giggles came, bringing tears to his eyes and a catch to his throat. He tried to turn to one side but could not find the strength. The thought that he was stuck on his back, flailing like an upturned dung beetle, set him off again. Guffaws hurtled out of his jaws and he crossed his arms over his chest to try and weigh them down. The last of the water ran out of his eyes and his belly finally settled down to rest.

The only sound he could hear was birds calling out to each other in a late afternoon panic. Kamal had fallen silent, the clapping and singing had died.

The sun began to sink, clouds of bats setting off towards the earth's sharp edge. He fell asleep and woke at points through the night: when his teeth chattered so hard that his head shook; when a creature slithered close to his ear; when a buzzing and droning seemed to engulf his face.

He opened his eyes just as the day's first pallor washed across the sky, his body soaked with dew. He could no longer feel the aches of the previous day. The poster of Kamal straggled into his vision, suspended in the flicker of an eye, her face blanching and then swimming back. He remembered the hysteria that had engulfed him and he sought the laughter again. Relaxing the muscles of his mouth, he thought of how funny it had all seemed. He smiled and let his breath out. The laughter came but it was not the same: this time it sounded thin and false.

MINU GOYARI DAY

According to the Best Children's Encyclopaedia, the deadliest volcanic eruption was in Tambora, Indonesia, in 1815. So much ash was hurled into the atmosphere that it blocked out the sun as far as Europe and America, temperatures dropped, crops failed, and people thought the world was ending. Ninety-two thousand died. But that is nothing, says the book, compared to the million or so that perish every year from the world's deadliest disease. Malaria has claimed more than three hundred million lives so far. The picture accompanying that fact is hideous: a giant mosquito, engorged with blood, sinking the blades of its proboscis into a patch of soft skin. He decides to skip the page about the world's deadliest reptile.

The power is out again today, so he can't go online. In any case, these days his mother is always first to grab the computer when there is a promise of uninterrupted electricity.

When he whines about it, she says: 'Just five minutes, shona. This is very important.'

He doubts that it is important and he is certain that it will not be five minutes, but he does not make more of a fuss. He is, in fact, very fond of the Best Children's Encyclopaedia, which he can carry into the cave he has formed in his bed. Pillows are piled high on two sides and covered with a navy blue quilt. The opening lets in enough light to read and he can run his toes along the quilt's satiny grooves.

His mother comes into his room, holding his canvas shoes, freshly whitened and with new laces. She is wearing the same sari as the day before and looks like she has not been to bed.

'Today is World Toilet Day,' she announces, as she puts the shoes into his cupboard. 'They have a day for every damn thing now. There is an International Donkey Day, or is it goats, anyway, some creature. There is a Smile Day, Party Day, Chocolate Day.'

It is only after she has left the room that he registers how strange her voice sounds.

Since his father's death, his aunts have told him that he is now the man of the house and must look after his mother. This terrifies him and he often looks to his mother to see if she shares this expectation. She does not ask him to do anything out of the ordinary, but he catches her looking at him sometimes in a way that seems to say her eyes will always be able to see him no matter where he is.

He does not want to be the man of the house. He knows that he is cruel, vicious and bad. He breaks things, hides them, throws them out because he can. Words burst out of his mouth and he is not able to stop them.

'You're not really my mother,' he says.

He ignores her for days.

'Will you cry at my funeral?' he asks her.

She is patient with him and laughs off the worst of his excesses.

'You're my lovely, loony boy,' she says.

'I'm not,' he thinks, 'I'm really not.'

The school van picks him up at the curve in the road, where he waits with Tina and her mother. He has always been afraid of Tina. She seems to be able to guess what he is thinking so he tries to be as impassive as possible in her presence, the features of his face held carefully in place. Tina often stands on a water drum, looking over the wall that separates their houses, into the top-floor windows where he and his mother live. Squat and solid, with thick hair that sits on her head like a crash helmet, she breathes heavily even when she is not moving, sharp gusts that are hot with knowledge.

The best thing about Tina is her mother, a gentle woman who always smells of freshly washed hair, who looks at him as if he is an injured bird and agrees with everything he says. He often talks about her at home, praising her beauty and her humour, until his mother stops smiling and falls completely silent.

The van screeches around the curve and slams to a halt. The door slides open and he and Tina hand their bags to the driver. Behind him, the seats are already swarming with children. The moment the door is shut, the van tears away.

They head towards the centre of Guwahati, passing Syed Uncle who is leaving for his silk shop in Fancy Bazar. He waves to them cheerily but nothing is what it seems with Syed Uncle. When he comes to the house, he is gentle and generous, affection streaming from his eyes. But in an instant he can turn taciturn and foul-mouthed, cursing the hill tribals he has to deal with, drunkards and terrorists he says, always wanting something for nothing. Syed Uncle is a Muslim and proud to be a true son of Assam: he has nothing good to say about the other Muslims either, the ones from Bangladesh.

'Bloody miyahs, always clamouring for jobs and spitting in the road. Every month, sneaking more of their relatives across the border, and if anyone asks they all pretend to speak Oxomiya at home,' says Syed Uncle.

He has heard this so often that the implication is clear: if you don't speak Oxomiya at home, you are an outsider. He is an alien because he speaks Bangla at home, even though his parents were born in Assam. He is not sure what that makes the Biharis whom he sees lining up by the construction site opposite his school, shy men with the eyes of children who look at him as if he is the adult, men who speak neither Bangla nor Oxomiya, men who don't appear to speak at all.

He tries not to think about this. But he knows that these differences can be a very dangerous thing. It is there in the words that flash up on the television screen and in the arguments overheard on the benches outside Ashirbaad Tea House. He knows it is the reason why his father was blasted to a pulp by a bomb as he walked past a bus stop several years ago.

His mother is hogging the computer again. She has been distant and brusque today, and he senses that any bellyaching from him will only have him sent out of the room. Instead, he tries to show some interest in her work.

'What are you copying down?' he asks.

'It's fascinating,' his mother says, 'the life this woman led.'

'Who?'

'Minu Goyari.'

'Who's she?'

His mother spins around, her eyes flashing.

'What do you mean, who's she? Don't they teach you anything in that school?'

He too wishes they taught him different things in school, but he stays silent.

'She was an amazing woman,' says his mother. 'A true heroine of Assam.'

She pulls him towards her: 'Come.'

He draws close and looks at the sad bags that have formed under her eyes in recent weeks.

'Minu didi gave up her life to bring together all the people who have been fighting each other in Assam. She was from a poor family in the forests near Gossaigaon, with many brothers and sisters. The only things of value they had were the silver bangles that her mother sold to educate her. She must have seen the signs of a remarkable future even in that little girl playing in the village.'

He nods as she speaks, looking at the dense print on the screen. His mind wanders. He has already lost interest in Minu Goyari and her silver bangles. His current interests lie much farther north and much further back in time.

He cannot stop thinking about Rasputin, his feral eyes shining out of every photograph, the beard that was taking him back to nature. He has read that the man was a lying crook, no better than the charlatans that loiter in Guwahati's bazaars. But he is unconvinced: this was a man who survived being poisoned, shot, strangled, stabbed and bludgeoned before finally being drowned in a river. More than that even, he had the power to enrapture a queen. There is a mystery about the relationship with the Tsarina that thrills and enrages him. The more he reads, the more it frets against the edges of his understanding. It is furtive, outrageous and exquisite: an obscenity that he cherishes because he thinks it is the truest thing he has ever known.

He does not ask his mother about his father and the circumstances of his death. He was not even a year old when it happened and he cannot miss someone he never knew. Occasionally, an image flares and then dims in his mind, a picture of a smiling man holding him high and drawing him close. The man is wearing a garland like the one that hangs from his father's photo in the hallway.

In any case, he has picked up plenty from family conversations: that the bomb was left in a jute bag, that there was hardly anything left of his father's body, that his carefully polished shoes were found on the other side of the street with hardly a scratch on them. He knows it would be foolish to confess it to anyone, but he mainly thinks of his father when he goes into Bata and sees the rows of lace-ups and loafers gleaming on their brackets all the way up to the ceiling.

He likes to handle his father's fountain pen with its delicate gold ridges and the camera lenses in their leather case. The names on his old jazz records fill him with delight because they are so much more gleeful than his own. Hoagy Carmichael! Artie Shaw! Hootie McShann! He has heard his mother mention Duke Ellington and when he sees one of his albums he is surprised to discover that the Duke is not an old man in a red frock coat with a sword slung by his side.

He hears his mother's voice, raised in anger. He is surprised because she rarely loses her temper and he did not know that anyone else was in her room.

'Ma,' he calls.

There is a pause and then she says something, loud but indistinct. He turns down the television and listens.

'There is nothing more to discuss,' he hears her say. 'I am entitled to my opinion.'

He goes to her room and pushes open the door. His mother is standing by the window and there does not appear to be anyone else with her.

When she sees him, she smiles and asks: 'What is it, shona? Did you want something?'

He shakes his head, looks at her for a moment, then at the empty room, and returns to the television.

A positive consequence of all the time she spends online is that he can pick whatever channel he wants to watch. He favours the nature programmes and is especially attracted to the documentaries that investigate life in the deep ocean. He has never seen the sea and is not interested in its surface: the thought of waves crashing on golden sands leaves him cold. He would rather know what the waters carry in their darkness. It is a world of beings that defy reason: fins, fangs and spines; plumes and tentacles; balloons of ooze that roll and dip without respite; and solitary spots that glow and fade. He wonders what would happen if a bomb were set off in those depths. Would it simply fizzle and fail under the weight of the sea or would it explode, sending columns of water shooting up to the surface, carrying their cargo of shattered skulls and spines?

The cold snap has finally ended and a school trip to Shillong has been arranged. They will be away for two days and one night – he is not sure where they will be sleeping, whether they will be expected to camp or if arrangements have been made in a dak bungalow. It is immaterial, as he is not going. He still occasionally wets his bed and his schoolmates' taunts would be unbearable if there were an accident on the trip. He would rather die, incinerated by the eruption of a volcano, struck down with malaria or swallowed whole by one of the world's deadliest reptiles.

His mother is not usually practical, she barely knows how to sew a button back on, but in a crisis she can have sudden inspiration. She takes the washing machine cover to her tailor and asks him to make a pair of shorts out of the plastic, slightly smaller than her son's PT shorts. She uses sticky tape to attach strips of old kitchen towels to the inside of the shorts. She throws the finished shorts against the wall to test their endurance. Then she presents them to him as her solution.

He is not convinced. He knows she would never try to humiliate him, but he searches her eyes for signs of mischief anyway. At last, he agrees to try them on. The fit is good, the elastic clings to his thighs and the padding is snug against his groin.

'How does it feel?' she asks.

'I don't know,' he says.

'Jump up and down,' she says.

He is too confused to refuse so he jumps. The shorts are secure and his heart begins to lift.

The next day the bus leaves Guwahati for Shillong, thundering past petrol pumps and the occasional stall piled high with pineapples and bottles of honey. They reach the sharp bends that slow the bus down, the forest closing in on either side. When they first glimpse Barapani, his friends leap to the other side of the bus for a better view of the lake. He stays where he is.

They are camping near the grounds of a school in the hills above Shillong, a clearing strewn with wild primroses. The food they are handed as they sit around the fire should taste of dew and stars, but he is not able to force any of it past his lips. And to drink would be to walk straight into ruination. His throat tightens. He can see the flash of fireflies all the way back to the blue hills in the distance.

It is finally time for bed. He is terrified at the thought there could be horseplay in the tent, headlocks and stripping, his jeans pulled down. Mumbling an excuse, he crawls into the tent before the others, furious that he relented, that he is here. He slides into his sleeping bag and zips himself up to the chin. He tells himself that all he has to do is stay awake, remain alert and he will be saved from shame. But his awareness falls away and sleep defeats him.

When he opens his eyes, the dawn light has made the blue of the tent turn a grass-green and the birdsong is loud and rich. It is morning. He starts and tries to remember what has happened, to determine if he is safe. He slips his hand under his waistband and around the seat of his jeans. He is dry. Unzipping his sleeping bag, he throws the flap to one side. He pictures his mother's face and a great cloud of love crackles and breaks over his head.

He is trying not to think about his mother, her new ways. She has spent the entire day on the phone, dialling number after number from a black book in her lap. He cannot hear what she says but the conversations are sharp and terse.

There are other things. She has begun to object to the windows on their floor being opened, saying the air is full of pollution that can flood the house and overwhelm their bodies. Their rooms are still and stuffy now, so he tries to escape to the balcony or to his uncle's part of the house. She has also taken to wearing a scarf around her neck, even when the weather is warm.

He wonders whether she is pregnant. He does not know how he has come by this information, but he is aware that pregnant women behave in strange ways. They burst into tears for no reason; they pace through the night; they gnaw at lumps of coal. But how would she be pregnant? His father is dead. The thought of a sibling, another child in the life he shares with his mother, fills him with dread. Everything would be tossed into the air, up for grabs. He would have to arrive at new conclusions about all the things that he has spent so much time resolving over the years.

He has to write an English composition for Miss Baruah on his hobbies. She is statuesque and witty, and he tries hard to gain her rarely demonstrated approval. Miss Baruah produces an exaggerated sigh of disappointment in the presence of her students, a slightly disgusting, moist sound. If he had to spell it, it would probably be: 'sthfffshhhkshhr'.

As far as he can tell, hobbies are pastimes that involve collecting things: stamps, coins, models – objects in which he has no interest. The only person he knows who collects anything is Tina's mother. They have rows of dolls from all over the world in a glass-fronted cabinet in their sitting room, sinister figures with rosy cheeks, straining out of their national costumes.

The other possible area of relevance as a hobby is sport. Cricket and football bore him and the only competitions he has enjoyed watching are the athletics at the Olympics. But it is not defensible to have a hobby that keeps him occupied only for a month every four years. So he concocts a passion for karate, scribbling down facts from the Internet and cautiously claiming only to be a green belt in the Shitō-Ryū school.

His description does not take him to the required word count so he adds a last paragraph, the only honest account in the essay. He writes that, on certain days, when banks of airy clouds rise up over the distant Brahmaputra, he leans out of the attic window, until his waist is resting on the ledge and he can feel the warmth of the roof tiles under his hands. He imagines that the clouds are the skyline of a city, with towers, bridges and citadels. Or that an armada is approaching, invisible sailors positioning the cannons on the warships as the sails billow. Or that a distant planet has sent its emissaries in a spacecraft to this crook in the map of Assam.

When his essay is returned to him, Miss Baruah has written in the margin: 'Looking at clouds is not a hobby.'

'If I get no response I will go and see them in person,' his mother says.

There is an embarrassed silence around the dining table. His uncle is picking fish bones out of his mouth, with a look of intense concentration. His aunt reaches for the water jug. He traces a spiral in the rice on his plate with a finger until his aunt smacks him on the wrist.

'None of them admit that our leaders have all failed Assam. But Minu didi understood, she knew that the question to ask is not about language or tribe or religion, but about the things that have disappeared from Assam over so many years, without leaving a trace. Where did all the tea go, the timber, the oil, she always used to ask, because we certainly have not seen one paisa from it,' his mother says.

The family remains mute.

There is one prawn fritter left. He wonders how long he should wait before reaching for it.

'They will never have seen a letter like mine,' his mother chuckles.

She has written to officials at a number of ministries, the letters copied to several media and civil rights organizations. It is part of her campaign to attain official recognition for the work of Minu Goyari.

'They will ask me who I am; who am I to plead Minu didi's case when even her own colleagues and family members have not asked for her struggle to be acknowledged. But it is precisely because no one else is doing it that I have to do it. I see that now,' his mother says, looking from face to face around the table.

'What has this Minu got to do with any of us? Why must you stick your nose into matters that don't concern you? If you are bored at home, there is plenty of work to do at the shop,' says his uncle.

His mother piles rice on to her plate, more than she will ever be able to eat, rice and more rice, a great mound, as if the act of spooning itself gives her immense satisfaction. He sees his uncle and aunt exchange troubled looks, but still not a word is said. Outside the dining-room window, the tangle of vines drops further, as their stalks begin to strain and snap under their own weight.

He follows Tina upstairs, feeling the banister's smooth wood against his palm. In the passage, the hands on the face of the grandfather clock shimmer like talons. They pad into the spare room; Tina shuts the door and draws the curtains.

'You go first,' she says.

'No, you.'

'Both at the same time then.'

He pulls off his T-shirt, the taste of metal in his mouth, as she begins undoing the buttons on the front of her dress. The room has wall-mounted cases that house the dolls that cannot be accommodated in the sitting room. Little cards hang from their necks, indicating their origin: Iceland, Uruguay, Malawi.

Tina has taken off her dress and is wearing a strange vest-like garment that sags over her chest and is tucked into her panties. He sits on the bed and wriggles out of his jeans, Tina blinking at each tug like he is getting it all shamefully wrong.

He knows that Tina is aware of his mother's capricious behaviour. She has also witnessed a recent argument between his mother and his uncle on the veranda. Two days ago, when his mattress was being carried on to the roof to dry in the sun, Tina was watching. She probably knows much more than he ever will of the circumstances surrounding his father's death.

He has to do as Tina says.

'Stand up,' she whispers.

He rises from the bed in his underwear. She puts her arms around him and squeezes hard, rubbing her hair into his face like an animal. He submits, slack and silent.

'Lie down,' she says.

He lowers himself on to the bed, looking at the poppies on the drawn curtains, their centres glowing darkly as they grasp the afternoon sun.

Tina clambers on top of him, their faces inches apart. Her breath is overwhelming: heat and reek and longing. He turns his face to one side to escape her mouth, afraid that she will laugh at his pounding heart. Most of her weight seems to be on his chest and he feels smothered.

'What's the matter?' she asks.

'You're heavy,' he says.

'Shut up, you're heavy.'

He prays that their underwear will stay on. He is electrified that this moment could be so close, that he is cruel, vicious and bad enough for it to be so.

Little grunts escape Tina as she nuzzles into his neck. Her writhing hurts him, pinching and squashing him in uncomfortable places. The tangle of her hair is in his eyes, wild and urgent. It is Rasputin's beard as he bears down on the Tsarina, holding her with his gaze and his knowledge. The Tsarina can't move her arms, she is frightened and stirred and dazed. Rasputin crushes her with all his might. The eyes of the dolls in the cabinet glitter as they watch Rasputin overwhelm the Tsarina.

'Get off,' he shouts and pushes Tina to one side.

Without looking back, he pulls the door open and runs down the passage to the landing. He leaps down the stairs three at a time, goes the wrong way and ends up in the kitchen. He turns back and scrambles towards the front door. It is only when he is fumbling with the lock that he realizes he is still in his underwear. It is too late to go back upstairs and claim his clothes.

As he emerges on to the front veranda, he sees Tina's mother unloading shopping bags from the car. He keeps going, racing down the steps and across the gravel path.

Tina's mother hears him and looks up.

'Oh my God, what's the matter? Did you hurt yourself, what happened?' she asks, tomatoes from a bag splattering on to the ground.

Tina's head pops out of an upstairs window.

'He pissed all over himself again,' she shouts.

It has been a week since Bijoya: the pandal has been taken down, the echoes of the chants and chatter have faded, and there is a pyramid of leftover sweet boxes in the kitchen. He is watching his aunt supervise the return of the special thalas to the attic, bundled in lengths of stiff cotton. All morning, rainwater has been gurgling in the gutters.

His uncle leads his mother into the room. Her hair looks like it does first thing in the morning, flattened on one side, chaotic and belligerent on the other. There is a large bruise on her arm and her blouse is ripped.

'This is just the beginning,' she says, shaking off his uncle's hand.

His uncle mutters to his aunt that they have just returned from the police station in Dispur and that he never thought he would see such a day.

She looks elated: 'I feel like I have really set things in motion. In my small way, I have added to Minu Goyari's struggle. They won't be able to ignore all her achievements now. I knew that they would try and intimidate me. That is what poor Minu didi suffered all her life. But the fight will go on.'

There are large patches of sweat under her armpits and her eyes are bright and fevered.

She was apprehended as she walked towards the Secretariat building, shouting slogans against the denigration of Minu Goyari. A knife was found in her handbag. She said it was intended for self-protection since she knew the police would become involved and she has read reports of their brutality. She was arrested for threatening behaviour and trying to start an unauthorized protest, a tamasha in the street that will be associated with the family forever. She is now out on bail, a feat achieved after his uncle called in many favours.

'All we want is some recognition of her struggle,' she says, lifting a thala and pressing it to her chest. 'All we ask for is Minu Goyari Day.'

He is told that his mother is ill: he will have to live downstairs with his uncle's family while she recovers. Two nurses are engaged, a sad woman with thinning hair who looks more unwell than his mother and a girl who murmurs into her mobile phone all day, shoving it into her pocket the instant anyone walks into the room.

His mother has gone quiet. She spends her days in bed or sitting in front of the television watching whatever is on. The computer has been abandoned. She asks him stock questions when he goes up to see her, addressing the area around his collarbone, smiling hazily at his answers.

'How are you feeling?' he asks her.

'Tip-top,' she replies.

He notices that she is putting on weight and that her eyes are retreating into her puffy face. She sleeps often and for long stretches.

He is pleased to have moved away from the top floor as he thinks this might help her recovery. What they need is a healer like Rasputin – someone who is able to look at her for just a few moments and discover what is wrong with her.

One evening, there is an urgent phone call. She had left the house to distribute handwritten leaflets about Minu Goyari Day and had walked into a main road. Cars braked, there was a dangerous skid, a man was thrown off a motorbike, a crowd quickly gathered. There would be another police case.

Family conferences take place without him. Voices drop and doors are shut in the middle of the day. He is shuttled out for tedious circuits of the park and then treated to ice cream, great drifts of vanilla and butterscotch that never seem to end. People gaze at him like he is always in the wrong place, as if he needs to be tidied up along with the magazines and the teacups.

'Your mother is very sick,' his uncle says, 'but we are sure she will get better. She needs to be in a special hospital where she can be looked after, with the best doctors and the best medicines.'

He thinks of all her unpredictable and embarrassing actions.

'How long will she be there?' he asks.

'Not long. We can go and see her whenever you want, and then in no time, she will be back here at home. Everything will be fine, just the way it should be.'

Weeks later, he is taken to see his mother. He and his uncle are in an unfamiliar neighbourhood at the eastern edge of the city. They walk through the low arch of an ancient building and sign a register on the ground floor. They are shown into a lift and, when the double grill is clanked shut, he is speared by the apprehension that they will never open again. The lift operator releases them into a dark corridor. Through a glass pane in a door, he can see a dormitory lined with beds, blankets thrown to one side.

'At this time they enjoy some fresh air on the terrace,' a nurse says.

They follow the nurse up a flight of stairs and emerge into the late afternoon, loud shrieks reaching their ears, stopping their hearts. They turn around and see that it is a monkey, wheeling around in a cage on one side of the terrace. There are other cages, some with more monkeys, some with parakeets that flounce and glare. High railings enclose the terrace and orderlies watch from the edges. Women walk in a slow circle in the middle of the space, an eerie orbit that makes him think they will suddenly disappear in a puff of smoke.

He spots his mother. She is not walking in the circle. She is sitting on a stool, looking at the sky. Her arms hang limp by her sides and she looks more content than she has seemed for a long time. He walks towards her, leaving his uncle staring at one of the parakeets, as if this is the real reason for the visit.

When she sees him, she smiles. She is just as happy to see him as she had been to see the clouds in the sky. He stands next to her and waits for her to speak.

The nurse walks past and ruffles his hair.

'Look how pleased your mother is to see you,' she says.

He nods.

'All the time, she talks about you and about Minu didi. Who is she, a relative?'

He does not respond. Instead, he sinks to his knees so that he is level with his mother. She lays her head on his shoulder and he feels her warmth flow into his body.

He turns to look through the railings at the city's rooftops as they spill down to the bend in the Brahmaputra. The orange disk of the sun dips a little more. The women stand still to plead with distant figures that drift along the banks of the river.

In later years, he will come to know some of these women by name. He will hear them talk of confidences they have betrayed, mysteries they have solved, intrigues they have uncovered. He will sit on a stool at the edge of the terrace, holding his mother's hand, listening to the parakeets and the monkeys as the sun prepares to slip into the river. He will be mistaken for a husband, for a son, for a spirit sprung from a stunned imagination. He will take his leave and promise to return soon.

He will think about Minu Goyari and he will carry out his own investigations into her life. He will visit public record offices and government departments. He will trawl cyberspace. He will scour journals, minutes and testimonies. He will write to scholars and follow up his emails with personal appeals.

'I am sorry to conclude that we can find no record of a person of that name who was involved in any major political, special interest or civil society organization,' will say a final communication from an academic at Cotton College.

He will remember his mother's scrapbooks, the collections of notes, cuttings and printouts that she catalogued with such care. He will return to his uncle's home and ask if he can look for his mother's papers among the detritus in their attic.

He will eventually find boxes marked with her name, carry them downstairs and spend weeks going through their contents. Along with photo albums, moth-eaten shawls and novels brittle with age, he will find the folders he is seeking. He will see news reports of insurgent campaigns and Indian army manoeuvres filed in no particular order. He will discover reams of unrelated articles on dying river life, nuclear non-proliferation and bee-keeping; clippings of cartoons and job advertisements; pages of handwritten notes on logging, drilling and estate management.

The tips of his fingers will be coated with the ink and the grime of his mother's fastidiousness. His eyes will smart from scanning the fine print. The dust of ages will dance in the air. But nowhere in the sea of material will he find a reference to a woman called Minu Goyari.

THE WORD THIEVES

As a child, Farooq imagined that adulthood, although terrifying in its proximity, would offer up the occasional consolation: the freedom to lock himself in a room with no prospect of intervention, an easing of his grandmother's authority, a few more inches of height. Now in his mid-twenties, he was grateful for his minor growth spurt and was in the process of reconciling himself to the other circumstances that had largely remained unchanged. He came when he was called and did what was asked of him to the best of his indifferent ability. He took the radio up to his grandmother's room when she yelled for it; he bought potatoes or mutton or tea on his way back from school; he beat the dust out of the rugs on the front steps, gasping and choking. Even most of the money he earned teaching was handed over to his grandmother without complaint.

Farooq's chest was narrow and sunken, an anatomical blunder. Acne bloomed on his face in a perpetual celebration of adolescence and, as if to counter this spree, his joints ached and grated through the day. His chin would have been weak but for the corresponding frailty of his jaw. A mass of smarting sinews and tendons, the short walk to school took him twice as long as any other person of his age. Any sudden sound, the clack of a ball on a stump or the thrash of a pigeon's wings, could make his heart stop and the light before his eyes dim for a second. On particularly cold days or on particularly hot days, he stopped in the shuttered doorways of shops until his nausea abated.

His brothers were hewn from different matter: tall vigorous men, with limbs like planks, fists like cudgels. They were continuously in motion, leaping, diving, scrabbling, their voices cannonading through the walls and windows into the narrow street beyond. Given these differences, there could reasonably have been questions about Farooq's paternity but his mother had been known as a devout woman. The brothers treated Farooq with a baffled kindness: they took on the chores that he could not complete, they trounced his innumerable tormentors, they made him laugh at their jokes and guffawed at what they perceived to be his.

'Why don't you teach the older boys at the secondary school instead of these babies?' Rafiqa Bano, his grandmother, would ask, thinking that a rambunctious male environment would fortify Farooq's character, give his chosen career some ballast, fill him out.

'I don't think I have the capacity for that,' said Farooq, the vision of such a bracing future turning his knees into halwa.

The little unformed ones were his natural constituency. He could set himself down in the middle of their bedlam and see only a serene bonhomie. He sympathized with the compulsion to cram objects into nostrils and to fill underwear with handfuls of mud and to watch with warm wonderment as urine sprayed on to bare feet. He did not countenance it but he comprehended. Much of the time he too longed to lie on the floor and bawl.

As he looked out of the window at the first snowflakes of the season, a delicate dance above the tangled mass of electricity wires and the weathered balconies of the buildings opposite the school, he managed to forget where he was. He imagined the sting of one of those snowflakes on the tip of his tongue, a tender nip that would disappear in a fraction of a second.

A scuffle broke out in the back row, a ferment of shoving and elbowing. Farooq shook his head at the agitators and waved one arm half-heartedly as a sort of threat. He looked to a spot in the far corner of the classroom where he had earlier rolled and stowed a cloth bag, there being no empty desks or cupboards in the room in which to put it. The thought of the bag sent blood booming into his temples and made his scalp sting with dread. He tried to focus on the lesson.

'What colour is the kite?' he asked of no one in particular.

'Blue,' came the cacophonous response.

'What colour is the fruit?' he asked, turning once again to face the bag.

'Red,' the children screeched.

'What colour is the bird?' he asked, his voice cracking.

'Green, green, green.'

In the months after the disappearance of Farooq's brothers, he and his grandmother exhausted themselves with speculation. They knew about the cells where young men were said to languish for years, facing one wall for months and then being allowed to face another. They tried to seal their minds from the vision of bodies buried in a grave at the bottom of a far-flung gorge. They considered the possibility that the brothers might have crossed the border one moonless night, their silence only a mark of concern for the safety of those they left behind. And on one occasion, they told themselves that the young men had left Kashmir and simply gone to seek out their fortune, to Goa, to Bangalore, to London. When they had achieved what they had set out to do, they would return to their kin.

Although she feared the worst, occasionally after completing her rounds of hospitals, check-posts and police stations in Srinagar, Rafiqa Bano would say: 'If they come back and I find out that they have been safe and sound all this time, I will kill them myself.'

She was a woman reputed for her ingenuity and foresight and when the conflict had begun in earnest, even though her two older grandsons were still children, she had begun to watch them intensely, informed by her knowledge of human nature and world history, of hot-headed youngsters in troubled regions, of the spark and flame of resistance. As they grew into strapping teenagers, she involved herself in virtually every part of their lives, demanding to know the names and family backgrounds of all their friends and acquaintances. She would sidle up to them if they were reading in their room and peer at the titles in their hands. She had no qualms about intercepting notes or letters left for them. On nights when there was no curfew she covered herself in a dark shawl and followed them at a discreet distance, retreating into shop doorways and behind parked cars, prepared for the wind that would gouge at her ankles.

And yet the brothers had disappeared, seized by persons unknown or having definitively given her the slip.

In any other family, the remaining son would have been under intense scrutiny, but Farooq escaped any such inquiry because it did not occur to Rafiqa Bano that he would do anything other than continue as he had always done: attend school, rub lavender oil into her temples and scrawl endlessly into his paisley notebooks.

In the darkness of his room, Farooq slipped the slim volume out of the cloth bag. It was an Urdu alphabet book, no different from so many others, a text of pastels, blocks of pink and cream and sky blue. More than a year old, its corners were hard curls, most of the pages creased or frayed, tea stains flecking several margins. The alphabet it contained was matched with images familiar to generations of children:

the letter alif and a pomegranate,
alif se anar;
the letter bay and a goat,
bay se bakri;
the letter pay and a fan,
pay se pankha.

And, finally, the letter zoi, which sat above the picture of a man with a stick,

zoi se zalim: a tyrant, an oppressor, a brute.

The book had been in circulation for many months before it came to the attention of a few vigilant law-enforcement officials. They were struck by the resemblance of the tyrant brandishing his stick to some of their own colleagues, a matter of grave concern in a textbook that would be studied by the suggestible young minds of the Valley. The matter was immediately taken up by senior officers and an explanation sought from the Board of School Education.

The response from the Board officials was emphatic. They insisted that the image was intended to represent a hooligan, a miscreant, a bad sort, and that any resemblance to uniformed police personnel was unwitting and a matter of pure hazard. They stressed that they were not stupid or reckless to go around insulting decent public servants; in other words, they had full knowledge of what was what.

The defence, although spirited, was considered thin and insubstantial. This was a clear attempt to subvert the state through an insidious scholastic route. The Board officials were charged with sedition, criminal conspiracy, defamation and provocation with intent to breach the peace, and all copies of the offensive publication were to be removed from circulation.

Farooq and a few of the other teachers had gathered in the school courtyard after receiving the news from the headmaster. The rumour was that an elite squad of paramilitaries was scouring market stalls and bookshops, storming into classrooms and libraries, with the aim of locating and destroying every copy of the seditious alphabet book. Rucksacks would be turned inside out, lunch boxes would be raided, there would be a rigorous scrutiny of playground barter.

The teachers passed the book around, flicking through the simple words and pictures. They considered the evidence. A man whose attire could have been a uniform. A luxuriant moustache. A bamboo stave in his right hand. An expression of boredom that could also be heartless brutality. Headgear that could have been a turban, a helmet, a cap, a bundle, a bonnet, a beret or a bandage.

They moved the image closer for a conclusive appraisal, trying to identify the locus of its insurrectionary power. One teacher said that the figure looked like a '70s Hindi film hero; another thought it was a Rajput warrior; a third a Maoist peasant; and the last swore, if he closed one eye, that it bore a strong resemblance to his sister-in-law Fatima.

There was no consensus on the exact classification of the picture, but the group was unanimous on one issue: 'The longer we stand here with this book, the more chance we have of inviting a hundred kinds of hell on our heads.'

In the safety of his room, Farooq looked again at the image. He smoothed out the creases on the page. The wise course of action would be to toss the book into a fire or rip it into shreds and throw it out with the eggshells and vegetable peelings. But Farooq gripped it with both hands and burrowed into his bedclothes. He pictured the muddled glee of his students as he read out words from the book, acted out images, corrected their handwriting. Fierce gusts rattled the panes of glass in the casement and the snow began to fall again. The ancient beams of the house let out a soft groan. The wind sounded like strange laughter in the dim light of the room, perhaps two brothers chortling at their own jokes.

As Farooq brought in the samovar, Rafiqa Bano leaned back against a cushion, her head touching the wall, as if expecting sounds of her neighbour Maimoona's avarice to filter into the room. The women had known each other for over thirty years: together they had attended weddings and funerals, haggled down traders in the markets, taken shelter when protests turned violent and made meticulous plans for the preparation of dozens of wazwans. When

Maimoona had tearfully asked to borrow thirty thousand rupees eight years ago, Rafiqa Bano had given her the money without even asking her what it was for. It was not a time for questions. Maimoona's son had just been sent home from an interrogation centre and he appeared in public only occasionally, always wearing dark glasses, his arm drooping at an awkward angle. From that time, even though their houses were only inches apart, eaves jostling in the narrow lane, the women hardly saw each other.

Farooq set down the samovar and looked at his grandmother.

Her ears were dead to the bubbling of the kahwa. She held her hands in a tense steeple in her lap, the yellowing nails just touching. Next to her, two glucose biscuits lay neglected in a saucer.

'You are driving yourself insane. Why can't you just forget the money? It's not as if we have a desperate need for it,' said Farooq.

'Be quiet, I'm thinking.'

'It's obvious that she does not have the money to return, so what's the point in worrying about it?'

'Shhhh.'

'After everything that we have seen, what is this money, what could it bring us?'

Rafiqa Bano lifted her head.

'Yes, the horrors we have seen. We know all about them. But that does not mean that other matters in life disappear, that obligations vanish. She still owes me that money and she would do well not to forget it. I trusted her like a sister but once she spent that money, she stopped coming here, stopped asking whether we are alive or dead. Yes, it may be a small thing. But even the small things have to go on. All these years, we have still been washing ourselves, hanging our clothes out to dry, putting food into our mouths, emptying our bowels.'

'What have your bowels got to do with the money?'

'How dare you speak to me like this? Can you not even show me a little respect?'

'You are the one who brought it up.'

'Why are you always talking about my bowels?'

'But you mentioned them first.'

'Allah-tallah I can't bear it any more. Take me away from this merciless world.'

'But listen.'

'Get out of my sight. I want to be left alone with the only one that cares about me.'

'Please.'

'Allah-tallah, take me today.'

Farooq could hear Rafiqa Bano's laboured breathing at the top of the stairs as she surveyed the articles she kept locked in a trunk. Boxed tea sets were crammed in with carved frames, copperware and crystal vases, all intended as gifts and keepsakes. But there had not been any weddings, grand festivals or birthday celebrations for a long time. In the last few years, the lives of grandmother and grandson had wavered and shrunk, like a large room reduced to its reflection on the back of a spoon.

She closed the trunk and went downstairs, leaning heavily on the banister. Farooq sat in a rumple at the foot of the stairs, his head in a book. She ignored him and went to the kitchen where she thought she had seen some mice droppings. If there were mice, it would of course be Rafiqa Bano and not Farooq who would have to deal with the problem.

Farooq heard the clatter in the kitchen, the opening of cupboard doors, the hauling out of plates and pots. The sounds seemed only to emphasize the indifference of the world around him. He began to seethe, his sunken chest doing its best to rise up in fury. This was all he had: the clean fragrance of a new book, the specks and swirls of the calligraphy, the comforting plonk of a word that landed in the right place. But now there were thieves at work, trying to deprive him of his only pleasure, alphabet pilferers, vocabulary bandits, plunderers of the lexicon, alive to all the perils inherent in onomatopoeia, the dark intents of alliteration, the jeopardy in rhyme. He saw his favourite phrases rolling up their mattresses, shutting their suitcases, handing back keys and queuing for trains and buses that would transport them to places far beyond the Valley.

He pressed the sharpened point of the pencil into his fingertip and watched the skin turn crimson. The grooves under his fingernail dipped and pinched each other and organized themselves into a new formation.

'Zalim,' said the demented lines on his skin, 'zoi se zalim.'

Rafiqa Bano returned, wiping her hands.

'No sign of the vermin today,' she said.

She looked at Farooq brooding into his lap.

'Sit up straight; stop hunching like an invalid,' she said.

Farooq grunted.

'Now what's the matter with you?' she asked.

'It's not fair, they are only doing it to be spiteful,' he said.

'That children's book? Again? Allah save me.'

'You don't understand.'

'What is there to understand? They banned this one, they will give you another one.'

'That's not the point. It's their madness.'

'Yes, fine. But you want to hear about true madness? Do you need to tell me about all the things that have happened here? What is your book compared to these real tragedies?'

'But it's just a book, for children to learn, and they want to take it away for no reason at all.'

'These children are better off perfecting their aim with stones and anything else they can find.'

'How can you say that? They are children.'

'Stop crouching there like a servant.'

'It's not fair.'

'For the last half hour I have been on my hands and knees looking for mouse shit. Where is the fairness in that?'

He turned away from her, hugging his knees, rubbing his toes against the rough surface of the rug. The sting of tears was very close – all it would take was one more stern word or one kind glance.

That evening, his appetite failed him yet again and he spent a disturbed night whimpering and squalling into his pillow. Jigar and Faiz chased him through the alleys of Nowhatta, declaiming verses at him, their hands grabbing at the fringe of the scarf that fluttered at his neck. Lal Ded, Arinimaal and Habba Khatun cornered him in the classroom and gave him the fiercest tongue-lashing of his life, always mindful of the metre and musicality of their invective. Mahjoor walked into his room, boxed his ears, asked him to smell the fragrance of a bunch of blush roses, and then boxed his ears again. When he woke in the morning, there was a humming noise in his ears that would not go even after he had cleaned them out with cotton buds dipped in soapy water.

It took Farooq several days to admit even to himself the nature of the thoughts he was entertaining. The moment of realization brought on a bout of diarrhoea so violent that he was soaked in sweat and wracked with shivers. When he finally emerged from the toilet, Rafiqa Bano gave him a look of profound suspicion. She said a prayer out loud, expressing the hope that he had not been masturbating. Then she sent up a further appeal that if this were the case, if he had violated the sanctity of his person, he be punished in terms that were severe but just, a lesson that the universe's moral code could not be trifled with even in a dank, windowless enclosure that received municipal water only for an hour every three days.

In spite of the fact that he was headed to a mohalla on the other side of the city, Farooq decided that it would be wise to take a few precautions. He had been growing out his beard and moustache for a couple of weeks and he had darkened the resulting wisps with a paste of diluted kohl. He had borrowed his late grandfather's glasses, the black frame barely able to contain the dense, wobbling lenses, a treasured memento that his grandmother usually kept swaddled in a stole at the back of her cupboard. He left the house, wrapped in an old shawl that concealed all but the top third of his face.

His journey through the city was a vision of cataclysm as he imagined soldiers bearing down on him at every street corner, gun barrels bursting through chinks in walls and booby traps sweeping his feet off the road. He got on a bus and ended up in a distant warren on the wrong side of the river. He took another two buses and finally arrived in the correct neighbourhood. As he tried to fix his bearings through the fog of his grandfather's lenses, a woman emerging from a medical shop peered at his get-up and he shuffled off into a side street, muttering like a lunatic. Opposite a row of garment stores, he walked into a gaggle of schoolgirls and nearly emptied his bladder. He crossed a ramshackle wooden bridge, the timber letting out a tremendous whine with each step. A convoy of army vehicles seemed to take an age to rumble across the next junction and he had to grab an electricity pole with both hands to keep from passing out.

When he finally arrived at the hardware shop, he was pale and exhausted. He had to wait to catch his breath before he could tell the man behind the counter what he wanted, a request that needed to be repeated three times. He managed to extract a roll of notes from his waistband without dropping them and was about to leave the shop when he bumped into Bashir Chacha, an old family friend.

'Farooq? Is that you?' he asked.

'No.'

'What did you say?'

'Yes, it's me.'

'What have you done to your face?'

'Nothing.'

'And what is the meaning of this shroud?'

'Nothing at all.'

'How is your grandmother?'

'All well.'

'And you?'

'Very well.'

'What's all this, renovations? And what are you doing here, so far from home?'

Farooq mumbled a khuda-hafiz and stumbled out of the shop, his legs bowed with the weight of his purchases.

'Do you know that boy?' asked the man behind the counter.

'Yes,' said Bashir Chacha.

'Very strange creature,' said the man, raising his eyebrows.

'He writes poetry,' explained Bashir Chacha.

Farooq hurried down the street with his bags, their straps cutting into his fragile fingers, his breath strained. A stray dog began to slink along at his heels, sniffing his bags intently, looking up at him with interest.

'Shoo,' said Farooq.

He dodged motorbikes and scuttled past rows of cheap watches and sunglasses laid out on dirty sheets. When he glimpsed the army bunker, with its high wall of sandbags and razor wire, he contemplated abandoning the whole enterprise. He was almost reconciled to collapsing in the street and leaving the authorities to do with him as they would, when the dog sidled up to him, cocked its head towards his bags and tried to lick his leg.

'Shoo,' said Farooq.

He scrambled on, past an abandoned temple, vegetable vendors dozing at their stalls and a line of khaki uniforms drying on a makeshift washing line. The dog continued to pad alongside, appearing to have concluded that their fates were favourably and inevitably entwined.

Farooq paused and pleaded with it for the last time: 'Shoo.'

The dog turned away from Farooq, lowered its haunches and ejected a curl of excrement inches from his feet. Farooq shuddered and scuttled into the road, tripping over a loose cable and colliding with a man carrying a sack of onions. On impact, his grandfather's glasses flew off his face and landed on the tarmac where they were instantly crushed by the wheels of a passing handcart.

Rafiqa Bano had spent the early part of the evening at the window, looking out for Maimoona on her way back from the bazaar. When Farooq raised his eyebrows at her, she lowered herself into the rocking chair and luxuriated in her disdain.

'She probably bought gold,' she said to herself.

'And a new fridge,' she added.

The two ate in silence.

After dinner, she watched the last third of a Hindi film, the news, a programme of crime reconstructions, the news again and a medical phone-in programme. It seemed to Farooq that she would never go to bed, that she would remain there for the rest of her days, solid and rapt, bands of light from the television flittering over her face.

He squatted outside the door, listening to the description of the next caller's protruding haemorrhoids, twisting the ends of his pullover around his fingers. Eventually, he heard his grandmother stir and he crept upstairs, listening out for more signs of her slow passage to bed. He waited until the rumble of her snores was loud enough before slipping on his pheran and picking up the packed holdall.

He was nearly there. He paused to rest, leaning against a wall, breathing out djinns that reached up towards the icicles that clustered over his head. Just visible at the end of the road was the faint shine of marble tombstones in a small graveyard. He listened for the sound of a patrol, picked up his bag and moved on. As he hurried past the Sufi shrine, he trailed his fingers along the grain of its green walls and touched his forehead. He had not accounted for the strain of carrying his materials through the dark streets, and sweat poured down his back under the many layers he was wearing.

Finally, he skirted a few patches of black ice, walked past the locked gates and set his load down on the ground. He surveyed the spot, ears trained. He positioned his torch with great care between two stacks of bricks so that it threw its beam in the right direction. In spite of the cold night air he was still perspiring, from worry, from exertion, from fear. He began work: measuring and adjusting. After about half an hour, he stepped back and looked in both directions. The light from the torch cast sinister rings over the lower half of his body and he had to pause every few minutes to squint at his watch.

The wind had died down but the air was still glacial. His limbs ached and he was sure that the cold was sloughing off layers of his skin. He wanted to drop to the ground and lie down in the road, even if it had to be on that vicious, freezing surface.

A sound that he mistook for the rumble of an army truck sent him ducking behind the pile of bricks. High-voltage shocks zapped through his heart and suspended his breathing. If he could have remembered any words of prayer he would have gabbled them, willing to make any vow, any sacrifice.

When he was sure there was no one around, he crawled back to his handiwork on all fours. The terror had energized him. He saw the faces of his students in the formation of the stars: Yasin's button nose, Imtiaz's sleepy eyes, Akhtar's perpetual scowl. He finally managed to summon a few ayats of his favourite surah, his head bowed. Smiling for the first time that night, he heard the gentle sound of what he thought must be the bare branches of the chinars clinking against the sky, adjusted the angle of the torch and stood up to complete his mission.

In the morning, by the time the sun was streaming over the ridges that ringed the city, a small crowd had already gathered opposite the school wall and an informer had dashed off to alert the jawans at the nearest checkpoint. A cock was still crowing somewhere as shop shutters began to rattle open. The smell of the day's first batch of bakarkhanis came drifting out of a nearby bakery. A wagon of walnuts was unloaded into a barrel. Women carrying firewood slipped into dark alleyways. Two jawans pushed their way to the front of the group, blowing their whistles and calling for calm. They stopped abruptly as they caught sight of the huge picture on the wall, its colours still fresh, its outlines uneven, drips of paint streaking the pavement in front of it: a moustachioed man in uniform holding up a stick, his face a crude smudge of fury. Zoi se zalim.

FIZZ POP AAH

We all thought Dad would be the first to go. These are the kinds of thoughts that dart through your mind on a busy hospital floor, leaving a pink flare of guilt in their wake. He is standing by the nurses' station, holding a stress ball advertising a pharmaceutical company, perhaps wondering how it is supposed to render its service: by being squeezed, ripped apart or hurled down the disinfectant-soaked stairs. None of these actions would suit my father. He is generally a man of peace, uninterested in sports and inclined to leave objects in their rightful place.

His health has been failing for the past few years. It is difficult to pinpoint the moment when a true decline began since he has never been a man of obvious vitality, fixed, I would guess, in most people's eyes as a clever, quiet man with slightly sunken cheeks and a tendency to wait too long before responding.

But the first physical sign may have been when we were standing by the carousel at the airport in Bombay. He spotted our suitcase, its surface studded with old Shakti-Cola stickers, and eased the trolley forward in preparation. He leaned down and heaved the suitcase up from the carousel, only to drop it on its side. Then he tried again, but lost his footing and was forced to lean on my mother's shoulder for support.

There have been a battery of tests over the years with many diagnoses, some contradictory, some bizarre. He was asked to blow into a pipe for as long as he could; then we listened intently although clueless as to what we should expect to hear. He was told to bounce a tennis ball against the wall and catch it but we knew that this would have been a challenge even in his sturdiest years. He walked in a straight line with his eyes shut; we watched in fascination. He stuck his tongue out and panted, rasped and yapped. Don't drink, the doctors said to him; don't run; don't lift; don't drive; and above all, don't worry.

Dad has been pretty good at following these instructions: apart from the driving. There a new stubbornness took root and the rest of us looked at each other in puzzlement. We watched him lean forward at an awkward angle and grip the steering wheel as if it were threatening to take off. We resolved that enough was enough when he turned into the no entry road behind the Shiva temple. So when it happened with him at the wheel, his foot pumping down hard on the accelerator instead of the brake, there was a certain inevitability about the lurch into the path of the oncoming van, the seconds of blackness, the scrunch of metal and glass.

I suppose it all began at the tail end of the seventies, just as we moved into the largest of the executive bungalows in the Shakti-Cola compound. It was a couple of years after Coke left India in a huff, refusing to reveal its famed secret formula. We were told that all foreign companies were imperialist demons: unscrupulous, unreliable and un-Indian. Home-grown industrialists began to take their place, puffed up with an ambitious piety.

Mr Eddie Edalji Engineer was one of their number. He had long planned to move into the food industry and here was his chance. He would create a soft drink to represent a renewed India, still trying to find its feet after the detonation of the Emergency.

He had in mind a product that would decipher the confused aspirations of millions of Indians, a tall glass, clinking with ice and pride, a sugary sparkle with which the multitudes could slake an unarticulated desire. His product researchers and market analysts came up with Shakti-Cola, a drink with immense power, sweeter than other sodas, but with a salty swash and a kick of spice. A mouthful of this was a gulp of what he saw as his compatriots' essential outlook: modern but rooted, traditional but rational, local but universal; not so much a thirst quencher as a stinging retort to any foreign condescension.

The Shakti-Cola logo would feature a sari-clad young woman, holding up a torch, throwing off rays of purpose and progress; she would be a world away from the roller-skating, sunglasses-wearing, bubblegum-blowing, disco-dancing youth that spread a different cola message.

We were among the first to arrive at the company's dedicated complex, carved into the green plateau of southern Madhya Pradesh. As the family of the finance director, we were entitled to one of the corner bungalows with two patches of front lawn, an excellent start in my mother's eyes. The plant was in place; the staff was rolling in; all that was required was permission from the government for production to begin, a certainty in the eyes of the well-connected Eddie Edalji Engineer.

But the era of the licence raj was still in full force and the extent of the bureaucratic obstacles and reversals took everyone by surprise. The planning regulators proved to be deeply hostile to the Shakti-Cola project: the country required steel and iron, not pop. Ministries passed files to secretariats, which passed them on to agencies, until they were recalled and passed on to sub-departments and then subdivisions. Bribes and favours disappeared into a dark void in Delhi. The Shakti-Cola maiden laid down her torch and held up instead a great web of unissued permits.

Eddie Edalji Engineer remained indefatigable, a man intent not on making a product, but on making history. His pockets were deep and his past successes fostered a notion of infallibility. Instead of admitting defeat, he asked for plans for the import of factory machinery to be redrawn to accommodate more advanced models.

For the managers' wives, having folded the napkins, laid out the china and warmed the soup, it seemed as though they were waiting for a guest that would never come. The patches of lawn in front of the bungalows dried out into crisp matting through the first April and May, then spewed and squelched when the rains came, and finally shimmered with a sad glow as the dew caught the winter sun. Careers continued to be mapped. The families attended film screenings and magic shows put on by the company. There were classes, clubs and coffee mornings. But still no cola.

At first, my mother seemed to love the social side of our lives. Her eyes were never brighter than when she was in the centre of a gathering, lobbing bold retorts, flattering the handsome, rallying the timid. She plunged into conversations even when they had delicately moved away from her side of the room. She was always the last woman to pick up her handbag and settle it on her shoulder.

But sometimes, my brother and I would catch her alone, staring beyond the kitchen window, talking to herself out loud, her mouth twisting into odd shapes, as if trying to pin down her precise outlook.

Mum would say that it was wonderful to have left the smog and scramble of a big city: life in our neat executive compound was safer, calmer, cleaner. Mum would say that the walls were closing in and that only people with no soul could spend their lives gazing at their colleagues' garden furniture. Mum would say that we were lucky to enjoy the protection and favour of Mr Eddie Edalji Engineer. Mum would say that we would all be better off at the bottom of a well.

Dad bought a second-hand Russian telescope and spent hours in the garden puttering around it, fiddling with the lens, adjusting the axis, tightening the knobs, and then looking at the sky, arms akimbo, as if waiting for a delayed show to begin. He started running, the heavy crunch of his tread sounding on the silent colony roads in the darkness of the early morning. When he returned, he always looked ragged and diminished, as if the endorphins had chosen not to exhilarate his spirit but to revive all the anxieties that he held deep in his heart.

Each month swirled into the next. The preparations for the beginning of operations at the plant had become the totality of the business. The executives were being paid; they had become accustomed to the anaesthetic comfort of life in the Shakti-Cola compound. They pushed their cufflinks through the stiff cotton at their wrists and got on the phone to Delhi.

In the meantime, my brothers and I settled into our roles as intermediaries between our parents.

'Tell Dad where it is. Tell him now before you forget.'

'If it's okay with Mum, go ahead.'

'What did he say? Were those the words he used?'

Little comment seemed to pass between them. The deadly calm of their shopping trips to the nearest town; the hush that settled in the sitting room between the time the curtains were drawn and the television switched on; the darting glance and the tired frown that passed for conversation: I don't know which of these silences Mum found the most difficult. I have never asked.

We are no strangers to this hospital: the mustard carpet in the reception area, the rattle of gurneys, the lifts that never arrive. The appearances from doctors are infrequent occasions of theatre. Rumours begin that they are on their way, they are in the building, they will be here at any moment. An administrator runs down the corridor holding a file. Dad puts his empty plastic cup in the bin, smooths down his hair. He expects the double doors opposite the lifts to snap back and a gang of professionals to wheel in like heroes. But the doors remain shut and the nurses blandly polite.

'Two minutes, sir.'

Dad reads the chart on the wall about good personal hygiene as if it contains a divine message.

When the doctors finally appear, light seems to stream into the corridor as footsteps echo in every direction and the certainty of recovery floods through the rooms.

The senior surgeon is tight-lipped and distant. He strokes the stubble at the back of his head and seems not to hear questions. From time to time he addresses statements to whoever is next to him.

'We'll need a CT scan,' he tells a passing cleaner.

'Get me Dr Sheikh's number,' he says to my brother.

The junior surgeon is full of information that he leaks like a punctured plastic bag. He describes what studies have shown, what the latest thinking is and what trials have taken places in Sweden, Switzerland and Singapore. He gives percentages, sample sizes and time limits. He has assimilated the content of many journals and conference papers. Families nod, inexpressibly grateful that he can speak so tirelessly about the transformative power of medicine.

The junior doctor's mobile phone rings and he answers it: 'Ma, sorry, can't talk now.'

The families stare: it seems incredible to them that he too has a mother.

When permissions for the manufacture of Shakti-Cola finally came through, there was a grand party in the community hall. Eddie Edalji Engineer congratulated the executives for their diligence and forbearance, inaugurated the executive swimming pool and sampled the sweets that each of the wives had made. As he prepared to leave, Mum spoke to him for over twenty minutes, beaming, virtually standing on her toes, hauled up by a sense of her own glittering self.

Production began two days later: uniformed workers began to file through the factory gates and press photographers arrived at the complex to record the moment. Coconuts were smashed on the steps of the administrative office and fireworks delivered in company boxes to the executive compound and the workers' quarters.

A week later, the families in the compound received invitations to a special screening, with instructions to be strictly on time. Dad would not tell us what we were going to see and we did not know if this was a consequence of his ignorance or a new waggish desire to surprise. We pulled up in front of the company auditorium, my brothers and I getting out of the car in a fevered state, our shoes gleaming, our long socks pulled up to our knees with the tops neatly folded down. We squirmed in our seats as the introductory speeches were made and all the rightful persons acclaimed and felicitated. The lights finally dimmed and the show began.

A man says goodbye to his wife and two children, his white shirt gleaming like ice, the parting in his hair seemingly positioned with the aid of a protractor, his hand gripping a briefcase. As he walks towards the gate, he picks up a few scraps of litter and, giving us a half-smile, places them in a bin. He walks to the bus stop where there is a neat queue. On the bus he offers his seat to an older lady. At the office his charming wave greets his colleagues, who by their dress reveal themselves to be sons and daughters of disparate parts of the subcontinent. The clock above his desk shows that he is five minutes early. He places his briefcase on the edge of his desk and gives it a half smile. He cheerfully receives a stack of files from a secretary and removes his pen from its stand. The hours spin round on the clock, files alight and depart, the pen dances in his hand. At the end of the working day, he closes his last file and gives us his final half smile. He gratefully accepts a glass full of ice from a peon, who also slides across a bottle of Shakti-Cola. The maiden on the bottle emerges into view like a goddess turning on the axis of the earth. Across the office his colleagues are communing with their own bottles, the peon is gazing at his drink as he sits on a stool in the lift, at home the wife is handing the children a couple of bottles from the fridge, crates appear in schools, restaurants and stations, spray shoots from bottles on to factory floors and car bonnets, sodas are held up in front of a village temple, on church steps, in sight of a glorious minaret.

And then a voice, itself like a cool, sweet draught, says with authority: 'Fizz. Pop. Aah. Shakti-Cola is refreshing the nation.'

'So, what happened?' a nurse will ask.

Dad has a few plasters on his face and arm. These minor wounds have been referred to as a miracle, given the impact of the crash. He does not even have a sling or a neck brace to show that he was in the accident. This is not a miracle, Dad says. A miracle is the sound of faint mewling under a pyramid of rubble a week after an earthquake, followed by a child being pulled out alive; it is a woman clinging on to a piece of driftwood in a freezing ocean; it is hostages escaping their captors. This is not a miracle.

'So, what happened?' another nurse will ask.

Dad will say briefly that it was an accident, a horrific collision that happened in a fraction of an abominable instant. But he will not say that he was behind the wheel.

To make up for this omission, he apologizes for other things. He feels terrible, he says, about all the time his family is taking up. He regrets the working conditions of the overburdened staff. He is so sorry for these toxic times that we live in, the pollution, the stress, the mayhem that bring the sick in droves to this hospital.

The nurse's name is Yasmeen. She travels to the hospital from Vanasthalipuram every day, a round trip of over three hours. Both her sisters are also nurses.

'My engagement got broken off two days ago,' she says.

'I am very sorry,' says Dad.

'I know. It's sad. I was really looking forward to giving up my job.'

'You shouldn't worry, you're so young. You will find another husband in no time.'

'His family said I was over-smart.'

'Really? You don't seem over-smart at all. I'm sorry, I didn't mean you don't seem smart. You look very smart, in fact. But not too much, you know what I mean. It is very strange that they said that.'

'They are completely wrong. If I was that smart I would not have got engaged to him in the first place.'

She leans forward and glances at the nurses' station but all is quiet.

She settles back down and they sit in silence for a couple of minutes, watching the images on the TV screen: a soundless cricket match being shown mostly in slow motion.

Then she says: 'These pictures on the wall, they are new.'

'They are very nice.'

'Do you think so? We hate them. Look at that one, doesn't it remind you of a giant insect yawning? And this one, I won't say what it looks like but you can imagine. I mean, this is a hospital, sir, full of people in pain, delicate people, and this is what we are showing them.'

'Yes, I see what you're saying.'

'The managers at the corporate office, they make all the decisions, even about what to hang on the walls. But they aren't the ones who have to look at these specimens all day.'

Standing up, she adjusts her belt and straightens her skirt.

'Be strong, sir, have faith,' she says. 'Everything will be all right. I have seen many cases like this where the patient has gone home absolutely safe and sound.'

Dad nods. If he could, he would apologize again.

Over the course of the next few years, we grew in stature as a Shakti-Cola family. The sight of the logo in a distant city would produce a pulsing rush of pride. When relatives came to visit, we drove them through the different sectors of the colony, along the pristine roads with their trim borders and showed them the giant Shakti-Cola lettering mapped out in purple and white begonias, the mini-golf course, the reservoir. My brothers and I boasted of the unlimited free bottles to which we were entitled; my mother boasted of the health care. We wore our Shakti-Cola caps to cricket practice, we ate our cheese sandwiches out of Shakti-Cola lunch boxes, we wrote passages on the formation of oxbow lakes with our Shakti-Cola pens.

The story was told of a number of villages in Chhindwara district where locals had come to believe that the Shakti-Cola maiden was an incarnation of Parvati. Shrines had sprouted for this new Coladevi who, it was said, had the power to reform wayward children and bring prosperity to desperate homes. Eddie Edalji Engineer could not have been more delighted.

Sales grew, capacities expanded. The product researchers and testers in the complex came up with new flavours: Mighty Mango, Absolute Apple, Luscious Lime. Bottling plants were springing up further afield. We hardly saw Dad who, as if to make up for the earlier inactivity, was mostly away travelling, working late into the evening or sitting in meetings, my brothers and I imagined, on something resembling a lifeguard's chair.

The husbands' career trajectories influenced the wives' social covenants. They joined camps, switched sides or simply retreated, at least for a while. Notions of competition, progress and popularity fell like soft rain over the executive compound. Casual judgements formed in one of the company's meeting rooms filtered back into all the managers' sitting rooms and kitchens.

'Mr Rajput is getting lazier by the day. Looks like a transfer is more and more likely. Oh God, the look on Sheela's face when she hears.'

'That new communications officer is very smart, definitely one to watch. But not if you're a woman. Those hands have been communicating all kinds of things to Miss Machado.'

'Mr Joshi can't even read a balance sheet properly. He is really only good to answer the phones.'

The weekly highlight was the Saturday evening party. These took place by rotation, lighting up a different house each week. As the evening wore on, the children had the same old fights, blocked a toilet and then ended up asleep in the hosts' bed, on the landing floor, in a cupboard emptied of all the linen.

Among the adults, as the evenings wore on, an excessive familiarity would develop, a reckless launch of bad manners, jokes that wore thin but were applauded out of a tired sense of play. My mother was the most active, weaving around the room, insinuating incompetence or predicting infidelity. It was all greeted with a group cheer that even a child could recognize as sham and bereft. My father would stand at the French windows, looking into the night sky, as if he had only just realized that he had forgotten to bring the Russian telescope with him.

And if the party was at our house, we would listen in our beds to the voices floating up the stairs on waves of cigarette smoke and perfume, the words lost along the way. Then, just before sleep snuffed out sound, my mother's voice, suddenly clear and sharp: 'Meena, stop hogging all the men, they might be interested in something we have to say too.'

Then it all began to go wrong. A strike hobbled production and plunged the company into years of litigation. One of the bottling plants was found to be using a contaminated water supply. Shakti-Cola's market share began to plummet. Eddie Edalji Engineer's enthusiasm for his brainchild began to fade with his advancing years. But above all, the Shakti-Cola maiden's powers began to fade in the face of her indomitable enemies. Coke had returned to India on the heels of Pepsi.

Dad's health took a turn for the worse. Mum pleaded with him to resign, saying that the moribund atmosphere of the colony was aggravating his condition. He would not budge; he would not be a rat; the ship was not sinking.

The stays in hospital began. My mother slipped into her role as carer without any fuss, but behind the façade the eyes continued to search. She engaged busy doctors in conversations about their time in medical school and she gave nurses advice on matters of household budgets. With Dad she displayed a fierce professionalism. Every now and then he tried, sadly, to catch her eye.

My brothers and I took it in turns to be around. We were animated and optimistic, bringing cards and board games, fruity anecdotes, a conviction that we could defeat the inexorable. In reality, we scanned the death announcements in the newspaper, looking not for the outré demise, the children who fell down manholes or the young men mauled by wild animals, but the slow decline of men of a certain age, their grainy images, a sense of the lives they had concluded and the things they were leaving behind.

Dad is still keeping his distance from the family. It is too soon for criticism or consolation. If he has to talk, he prefers the company of nurses, benign strangers who see someone else when they chat to him. Only occasionally will he be drawn into a conversation with the relative of another patient. The woman sitting opposite him has been putting mints into her mouth all morning, cloudy lozenge after lozenge picked from a large family pack in her lap.

'How is your sister today?' he asks.

The woman stops chewing and says: 'They told me she is stable. I don't know what that means. Do you?'

'I think it means she will get better, that the dangerous phase is behind you.'

His voice sounds false and contemptible even to him: he knows that the cancer-stricken sister has been seriously injured in an accident. It is horror bearing down on horror.

'We'll see,' she says, crunching down again on the mints.

Dad looks uneasy and begins to massage his arms. He tilts his head as if he is listening for a clue in the air. He stands up and shakes his legs to see if this will help. It does not, so he sits down again. Then he recognizes the feeling. He is hungry. He has not eaten for many hours. But he still won't eat. It is only the beginning of his penance, the least he can do.

'They made my husband piss into a funnel.'

'They made my husband piss into a pipe.'

'My husband pissed in the car.'

Outside, it could be day, it could be night, there could have been a blizzard or a sandstorm, or a marauding beast flinging cars into buildings and laying waste to Nampally Station. Inside, there is only the powdery blue gleam thrown off by the hospital lights.

A nurse walks past, fanning herself with a patient's notes.

'She is going to be a vegetable for the rest of her life,' says the man in the dark glasses to his wife.

Dad shifts along the sofa, away from the couple.

His face seems to ask: 'What kind of talk is that?'

And indeed, what kind of vegetable? An aubergine: fat and shiny, bristling with accusations, purple with anger. Maybe a cabbage: simple and serene, lying in gentle folds, growing paler and softer by the day. Or a potato: cold, hard and grey, grimly hanging on but determined not to show a single sign of life.

An administrator walks up to Dad and leans down with her hands on her knees, as if she is talking to a cub in its cage in the zoo.

'Please, sir, if you don't mind, I need those insurance details again,' she whispers.

Dad hands her a card from his wallet and sees the photo of Mum, a headshot taken thirty years ago when her hair was parted in the middle and fell in tiered waves over her shoulders. Her eyes are out of focus, making her seem a little vulnerable, maybe even on the margins of sanity, a look that is completely uncharacteristic. Is that why Dad picked this photo?

He stares for a moment and then snaps the wallet shut.

We have not been left a single trace of Shakti-Cola. None of my younger colleagues have ever heard of it. No one reminisces about it. Retro fashions have ignored it. There is no wall in a small town bearing its outline, no palimpsest where the logo is detectable in spite of coat after coat of white paint. The satchels, the umbrellas, the key chains: all gone. Even the stickers on my parents' suitcase have disappeared, scratched off by Mum or simply worn into little fragments that curled away in a foreign land.

The digits on the wall clock blink: it is four in the morning. The water cooler is empty, a bulb has blown at the end of the corridor, there is no paper in any of the toilets. Sweet wrappers and magazines are strewn all over the table in the waiting area. The phones are silent.

The morning bustle begins soon. Nurses check on patients, breakfast trolleys arrive, drugs are handed out. Dad goes down to the canteen and stares at the items listed on the board as if he is encountering them for the first time. The glass case is empty apart from a piece of chocolate cake that was there the day before.

He finishes his breakfast and returns to the waiting area, looking around to see who has arrived, who has left.

Therapists are helping an elderly man to walk.

A porter replaces the blown bulb and murmurs a joke to the nurse at the station as he leaves.

And then it's all over. Although, in fact, this is just the beginning. A doctor approaches Dad and puts a hand on his shoulder. A nurse shakes her head. My brother goes into the stairwell to phone other members of the family to let them know.

There is a silence, a stillness that closes around its own empty core. The door of the room opposite swings open and out floats a child's voice, absorbed, satisfied, giggling. The laughter fills the quiet corridor. It is a relief to hear that sound and what it says about the wild, wasted future.

We arrived at the crematorium in a straggly procession, the men getting out of the cars and standing in self-conscious contemplation on the barren ground. The wind was loud and unruly, and when the priest's voice rose up, it seized whole phrases from his prayers, leaving only a sketchy staccato dissonance. It was hard to believe that the words came from the mouth of a living man. Crows landed on the walls, one after another, ruin reflected in their eyes. Inside the squat building all was dark and silent, heavy with the dread of heat and obliteration.

As the mourners began to drift away, my brothers arranged to pick up her ashes the following day, the naturally grave and reflective set of their faces making them somehow suited to this task. They wore the same look they would wear when being told off as children, a look that suggested they were tackling complex mental arithmetic. They got into the car and made sure that Dad was properly strapped in. For a minute we all sat there, watching the tinges of evening slide down over the windscreen.

Now the lights are coming on in the city as we make our way home. Beams shift through the violet air on the highway and shimmering columns plunge one after the other into the waters of Husain Sagar. The street lights form a chain in the haze and a long gleam shears up the steel rim of a high-rise. Glittering particles buzz and sing above the traffic.

The car is hemmed in on all sides. Vendors weave through the gridlock, holding out trinkets that sparkle or dance or chime. Dad lowers the window, raises it, lowers it, until my brother puts his hand on his arm. Then he stops. The red changes to green and back to red but the car only moves forward a few inches. Suspended over the chaos of vehicles, the advertising hoardings are lit by a powerful glare, oblongs that offer indistinct attractions, images that seem to sway in the air. The largest screen comes slowly into focus: a boy raising a soft drink to his lips, headphones clamped over his ears, eyes closed in anticipation, silver droplets beading the bottle, the condensation about to drip slowly on to his face.

Acknowledgements

All my thanks to:

- everyone who read and commented on the stories or helped with research – Arshia Sattar, Faiza S. Khan, Ashutosh Bhardwaj, Nitoo Das, Fahad Shah, Lisa Smith, Michael McMullen, Martin Roseveare, Priya Kapoor, Stefan Kamboj, Natasha Davis and Richard L MacDonald;
- Tara Gladden for copy editing the manuscript;
- Jonathan Pelham for the cover design;
- Ajitha G.S. at HarperCollins India for her careful editorial work; and for all their support, Karthika V.K. and the team at HarperCollins India;
- my agent Priya Doraswamy for her continued generosity and enthusiasm;
- Karen Maine at Daunt Books for her fearless and vital editing;

– Laura Macaulay at Daunt Books for all her invaluable work on the manuscript and for her faith and support from the very start;
– my parents and sister, Mamta, for everything that has gone into this book and so much else;
– K.J. Orr, for many kindnesses and for showing me, with great precision and great humour, what to expect from a short story; this collection is dedicated to her.

Notes and additional copyright information

'Eternal Bliss' was shortlisted for the Bridport Prize.

'Drums' was shortlisted for the Commonwealth Short Story Prize and the Zoetrope All-Story Short Fiction Contest.

'The Agony of Leaves' was previously published in *The Baffler*.

'Hero' was previously published in *Prairie Schooner*.